book one in the
Father/Son
duet

LIKE
Father
LIKE *Son*

Leigh Lennon

Like Father Like Son
Copyright @2019 Leigh Lennon

Editing by Ellie McLove
Proofreading services by Deaton Author Services and The Formatting Lady
Pre-Proofreading by Horus Proofreading
Formatting by The Formatting Lady
Cover design by Najla Qamber
Photographer: Eric David Battershell
Cover Model: Chris Spearman
Alpha Reader: Emma Albright
Beta Readers: Nancy George, Kymberly Dingman and Kelly Green

ISBN: 9781080787029

Like Father Like Son

I said good-bye to my son. But he had one final request—a
letter I'll never forget.

Dear Dad,
If you're reading this, it means I'm gone. I had one
dream, growing old with Holland. Death won't stop me
from providing for my wife. And because you're the
best man I know, what I'm about to ask—my last
request—I know you'll do. Please take care of Holland.
Take her back to California with you. It's a lot—I
know. But, I'm placing my most precious possession in
your hands.
Love,
Scott

But the thoughts swirling through my mind are certainly
not what my late son had in mind. How do I resist this
woman in front of me?
After all, you can't choose love, it chooses you.

DEDICATION

To my many friends who listen to my book ideas over and over again and smile through it. Thanks for accepting me for who I am and all the craziness that surrounds me!

To the one person who taught me if you were lucky to find love, accept it and live your life for you! I wish you had been able to read one of my books! I know you would have been my number one fan. I miss you every day Mom. I love you!

LIKE FATHER LIKE SON PLAYLIST

Maguire's Play List
Bon Jovi, "Blaze of Glory"
Bon Jovi, "Blood on Blood"
Bon Jovi, "Livin' on a Prayer"
Bryan Adams, "Summer of '69"
Guns N' Roses, "Welcome to the Jungle"
Metallica "Enter Sandman"
Metallica "Nothing Else Matters"
Mötley Crüe, "Home Sweet Home"
Poison, "Every Rose Has Its Thorn"
Queensrÿche, "Silent Lucidity"

Holland's Playlist
Death Cab for Cutie, "I Will Follow You Into the Dark"
Fall Out Boy, "Centuries"
Fall Out Boy, "Uma Thurman"
Panic! At the Disco, "Say Amen"
Sunny Day Real Estate, "Pillars"
Taking Back Sunday, "This Photograph is Proof"
The Front Bottoms, "Flashlight"
Weezer, "Buddy Holly"

The Author's Playlist

Coldplay, "Yellow"

Creedence Clearwater Revival, "Fortunate Son"

Ed Sheeran, "Castle on the Hill"

Green Day, "Wake Me Up When September Ends"

House of Pain, "Jump Around"

Kid Rock, "Warrior"

Jo Dee Messina, "Heaven Was Needing a Hero"

Lee Brice, "I Drive Your Truck"

Little Big Town, "Boondocks"

Luke Bryan, "Drink a Beer"

Matchbox Twenty, "3AM"

Rednex, "Cotton Eye Joe"

Tim McGraw, "If You're Reading This"

Toby Keith, "American Soldier"

LIKE
Father
LIKE *Son*

PROLOGUE

Sixteen years earlier

I kneel on the hot California cement when his large hazel green eyes fill with water. His flushed fat cheeks are only a couple of things on his small face that have my two hundred and ten-pound body wanting to smash something. He's clinging onto the Curious George stuffed animal I bought him for his first birthday.

I ignore the incessant tapping of the she-devil herself standing behind us. Not only is the tap-tap causing me to want to jab an ice pick through her Botox lips, but her annoying noises can't be contained to just her fingers. Long moans even make my little guy a bit more uptight, clinging onto me like his life is about to be torn to pieces. *And it is.*

"Listen, Sport." My nickname for my son isn't overly original, but the second he could walk, he had a soccer ball, basketball, or football in his hand. The kid, at only six, has natural skills that I want to continue to instill in him. But, that has all gone to shit.

But now, my time will be condensed to two weeks at Christmas and a month or two during the summer. As much as I fought for custody of my son, and I fought like hell, Christine convinced the courts that after our divorce, she had been left destitute and without a way to support herself. She put on quite the performance with the judge insisting that being around her family would be the only way to get on her feet after such an awful separation. Her infidelity didn't sway the judge and he claimed we had equal rights as parents. And though that's what the law claims, my lawyer warned me that unless the mother has been negligent and we couldn't prove the move would be unsafe for Scott, he would most likely side with the mother. And fuck, she should have been awarded an Oscar for her performance of a decade.

"Daddy, I don't want to move to Virginia." The tears in his eyes flow down his face. My own face turns to the bitch I thought I once loved.

My eyes plead with her. "Christine, please don't do this," I mouth where she can see me, but Scottie can't.

"Scott, honey, we have a long drive. Say goodbye to Daddy." She slips into the seat of her beat down Jeep. The idea of my Scott driving cross-country in this vehicle has me more nervous than not seeing him as often as I had when Christine only lived five miles down the road.

His long arms find passage around me, and he's not letting go. *Yeah, buddy, I don't want you to leave me either* is what I'm thinking.

"Maguire, c'mon. We've gotta get going. Please, can we limit some of the dramatics? For fuck's sake, y'all are men, not sissies."

Christine's southern accent she's tried for years to tamp down seems to seep from her lips when she's on bitch mode. With her talking to both Scott and me in this way, bitch mode is in overdrive.

"Alright, Sport, let's get you in the car. You and Mommy are going on an adventure. Don't forget, I'm flying out to see you for a week before school starts. You and me, we'll go camping along with so much more."

I lift him up and buckle him in his booster seat, giving him one last kiss that will have to hold me for two months. We were used to going to the park after work each day to dribble the soccer ball or sometimes I'd put him on my shoulders while he dunked the basketball.

It's all up in smoke because Christine has decided after the divorce, Scott's extended family should be more of an influence on him than his own father. In her manipulation, she's taking away my right to mold him into a responsible young man. This has been my dream since his small little body had been placed in my arms.

I shut the door, one last time taking in his sweet little face that imitates my own. The pain that's coursing through my body is physical, and all I want to do is grab him— keeping him with me like he should be.

I don't want to talk to Christine, and when I turn my back, she calls out to me, "M, hold on a second." Gritting my teeth, I twist my body toward her, holding my own tears until my son is gone. "I'll have Scott call you each night when we are snug and safe at a hotel." She adjusts her rearview mirror while biting her lip. This is never good; it has always been the one way I'd been able to tell when she's lying. It's how I found out about all her affairs, of course, that had been after I caught her in our bed with someone else.

"What is it, Chris?" I probe.

"Mama is planning on taking Scott to the beach the weekend you were fixin' to come out. Can you come a different week?"

I slam my hand on the open window door. "No!" Scott begins to cry louder, and I have to contain my temper unless I want his last memories of me to be his mom and me fighting.

I lean in closer to Christine, where only she can hear me. "I've given up most of this summer with him so he could get settled. I have my tickets and it's already approved with Ned. Don't challenge me on this," I threaten but with her lips pursed, as it is when she's hell-bent on getting her way, I understand this subject will be revisited another day.

I make my way around to where he's buckled. Leaning in, I kiss him on the forehead one last time. "Okay, Sport, be good for your mommy. I'll talk to you tonight."

Christine pulls out, and I watch the taillights of her beat up Jeep until it turns the corner four blocks down the road.

CHAPTER 1

Present

The day I left that podunk town and became Mrs. Scott Jameson Parrish is the day I compare all days to. Sure, a woman's wedding day is supposed to be all wonderful, and it was, even if we were only at the justice of the peace. But every day I can spend with Scott as my husband marvels the next.

No one had prepared me to be a military wife—a young military wife at that. Scott was only nineteen when he married me on my eighteenth birthday. My daddy would never have agreed to me leaving the farm so young if I wasn't legal. It had more to do with losing some of his valued labor than losing his daughter.

Leaving Rustburg, Virginia for North Carolina was not only the best thing we could have done, but it was essential. Scott's own mama is the bee's knees at manipulation and tried like hell to break us up over the years we had dated. She always wanted him at her beck and call.

With little but the clothes on our backs and our marriage certificate, Scott had joined the military and we were making it work—even if we were away from one another longer than together for the first three years. And he had been home on leave for two weeks—where we barely made it out of bed.

The next three months would be lonely, but I've become fast friends with several other wives whose husbands are in Scott's unit. Three days is all it has been since hearing from my man. I'm in my own little world, sewing curtains for Sarah. She's my neighbor and best friend who has found out she's expecting a little girl. I've picked out pink and purple unicorn fabric. Sitting at the sewing machine Scott bought for me, I'm about to start work on these darling curtains. Sarah had not been surprised at my choice since I'm always telling her unicorns are my spirit animal.

A loud knock pulls me out of my world. Sarah frequently comes over this time of the morning with two cups of coffee in her hands. I keep telling her I hate it and she insists she'll make me a coffee drinker eventually.

Opening the door, still in my bathrobe, I have bright purple fabric colored unicorns I'm pinning when my eyes dart up because I don't smell the java that usually permeates my nose. It takes a second for all the pieces of my perfectly planned life to come undone at the seams. My husband's company commander stands in front of me, along with the chaplain. With them, is a man I'm too familiar with—any military wife's nightmare—standing at the threshold of our government issued house. Captain Hillier, the casualty assistance officer, has made it his mission to know every spouse of his soldiers. The officers don't have to say anything. If these three men show up at your home in their dress uniforms, no words ever need to be said. He catches me before I fall. I'm kicking, screaming, and yelling when all the other doors to our cul-de-sac open and I'm surrounded by wives who fear the same visit from day to day. But it's not their husband who has been killed in action. It's mine.

It's the third time I let *her* call go to voice mail. It's funny, our kid is twenty-two, and I stopped shelling out any more money to the crazy bitch the day he graduated high school.

My life as a dad had not been what I'd imagined it would be when I held him for the first time. We weren't geographically close. Christine made sure of that. As Scott grew up, each year until he was thirteen, it was met with, "I want to go live with Dad."

I'm sure it hurt Christine to hear his words and I never pushed him. As a matter of fact, I'd tell him, *Virginia is an excellent place to live, Son. You have so much family surrounding you.* I tried to make things easier for Christine, never understanding why. Oh, yeah, I love my kid and part of being a parent is sacrificing.

But each year, Christine would tell him, "If your dad really wanted to be a part of your life, he'd move to Virginia." I never found this out until his words wounded me one night, one of the last times he visited me for summers when he was sixteen. By then, he had a serious girlfriend who he eventually married and summers at my house became a thing of the past.

And the truth be told, I wanted to move to Virginia, solely to be there for Scott. I had busted my balls to make it happen. Christine strapping me with such high alimony and child support is one reason I couldn't move. Plus, a year before I caught my cheating whore of a wife with another man in our bed, I'd bought into a partnership in a new business. Seventeen years later, we're very successful, but it has taken time to build.

As Scott had gotten older, Christine hemmed and hawed over holidays. I rented a cabin for a month in June and December to be closer to my boy. I would fly out a couple times a year for big games. And he'd come to visit me, too. We made it work, but the resentment lived deep in him thanks to the manipulative words of my ex.

The phone keeps buzzing when Irene, my assistant, pops her head in my office. "Maguire, sorry to bug you, especially for this. Christine is on the phone and claims it's an emergency."

"Shit." I'd hoped to have avoided her most recent rant. The funny thing about Christine, she had gotten married the day after alimony had stopped. She cheated on me, but I still got saddled with paying her twelve hundred dollars a month in alimony alone for eight years, not to mention the child support I paid until Scott graduated. She's been through a couple husbands since then, and quite honestly, it's too much to keep up with.

I pull at my corded landline hard; I'm surprised I don't yank it from the set itself. "Chris, what the hell is so important you're blowing up my line like you blew up our marriage?"

Yeah, I'm usually not a dick, but when it comes to her, I'm one to the tenth degree, if not more.

"Maguire?" Her sobs fill the line. "Maguire…" I can

barely understand her, but she's called me enough over the years sobbing, asking for a second chance. I can decipher her need by the mere tone in which she uses my name. It's soft but rushed. Slow but frenzied.

"Chris, hell, I don't have time for this." I'm close to slamming the phone down, ending this call.

"No, no, it's not…fuck—Maguire!" she yells, and I take the set from my ear for a second when the crying intensifies. "He's gone, M." She hasn't called me M in years. "He's gone, gone, gone, gone."

My breathing grows heavier and my *patience is gone* if she thinks I care about her latest fling leaving her high and dry. "Who is it this time and how much money do you think you're getting from me?"

"M, listen to me." She's begging now, and for the first time, she has my attention.

"Okay, I hear you, Chris, who is it?"

"He's gone, M. Our boy is gone. Scottie, he's been killed in action."

I drop the phone and all I hear around me is a massive crash as both Ned, my business partner, and Irene, fly into my office.

CHAPTER 2

Grief—it's an unpredictable shit show. It's an emotion of hurt manifesting itself into something so fucking physical, the pain has me gasping for air. The idea of burying someone who is a piece of my body and soul—it's like I'm in a bubble. I no longer feel as if I'm in the world around me, and when someone speaks, it sounds muffled.

Ned flew with me to North Carolina. I could barely function. I forgot what key unlocked my front door. I had sat on my bed—with a tie in my hand, unable to remember what I had been doing. It was only when Ned and Elise, his wife, arrived and found the front door open with my eyes heavy, that my mind finally played catch up.

Elise had to pack for me while Ned made the arrangements. It wasn't until I was on the plane did it fully hit me. A man, my size, crying like a baby in a packed confined space, had to have been a sight for many. Even the air marshal got involved once, thinking I was some flight risk, about ready to go postal on everyone.

I'm now face-to-face with the casket. My mind is still

clouded, I'm not even sure how Ned and I have gotten to the funeral home. Renting a car and getting our luggage are all events I can't remember. It's only when I enter the room with his body; I finally understand where we are.

Christine flies into my arms and we both hold each other. I hate the woman ninety percent of the time, but at the end of the day—Scott is, well, was, a part of us. We created him, and this loss is only something the two of us can understand as parents.

But so much is out of our control. Scottie, who would always be ours, isn't ours to fully mourn together. Christine's words race around in my mind, about his wife and all the arrangements she's not letting Christine be a part of. It's so much to take—the casket next to me and Christine's incessant complaining, which I haven't missed. It's then, a girl who looks maybe sixteen, if that, enters the room for family only, by herself. Christine pulls away from me, muttering something about wanting to bitch slap someone, storming out of the room. I should go after her, but my mind is on the girl child near us. She deserves to be here as much as Christine or myself. I'd only met her a couple of times during my visits with Scott, but there's no denying the anguish filling her puffy eyes.

"Mr. Parrish," she begins, stopping a foot from me, her eyes fixed on the casket. "I'm not sure if you remember me."

"Holland, yes, of course, I remember you, darlin'." I look at her picture—hers and Scott's—every day when I grab my keys from my desk where their wedding picture is placed. But what can I do for this virtual stranger who shares my same last name?

Her hair is light brown with bright purple ends. She's wearing a skirt decorated with pink flamingos and a bright green sweater. There's no way I can miss her. Maybe grief messed up her color palette as it had with me and my tie. There's more to her than her loud clothes and dyed hair. She's so tiny. Compared to Scott, he had to have towered over her. Her face is narrow with high cheekbones. With bright red lipstick on her lips, they are full. I notice this as it begins to quiver.

She clasps her hands together, her chin falling to her chest. I don't see her eyes, a color I can't tell as her tears fall quickly. She's quiet, still looking at the floor. "Holland, darlin', are you okay?" What the fuck am I asking, of course, she's not all right and on top of it all—she has to deal with Christine.

Her eyes pop up and a forced smile covers her face. "Um, I'm so sorry, Mr. Parrish. I mean, this isn't just my loss." As soon as she looks at me, she turns away. "You look so much like him. It's uncanny."

Yeah, she's right. Scott, from the day he was born, was my twin. Christine used to call me and complain about his attitude as a teen, swearing he was too much like me.

"Um, yeah, we get that all the time." I stop when I speak in the present tense, and it hits me all over again—I won't get this compliment again, about my son looking like me. It won't be *we get*—it will be *we got that all the time*—when he was alive.

The flood of emotions come and go in the twenty-four hours I've lived with the understanding that I'm now a bereaved parent. Hell, I'm a parent without a child. I turn to the closed casket where Scott is in the room with us. He's unable to tell me to stop. He'd only want me to take care of his wife.

I try to steady myself, but I can't, and I find the nearest chair in the room to sit down, my head between my legs. Tears fall from my eyes as they have with Holland. But then she grabs my hands, kneeling in front of me. "Mr. Parrish, I can't even imagine." Her kind eyes are a deep brown, almost black. With a small tip of her lips, her apology is heartfelt.

"Oh, darlin', I should be..." What should I be? Stronger? Here for her? I barely know her.

"No, Mr. Parrish. He's your son. I know you didn't see him much, not as much as you two would have liked but..." she stutters, taking in a deep breath. "He adored you, respected you, and only wanted to make you proud." She places her hand over her heart, visibly shaking.

Did he ever wonder anything else about me? I couldn't have been more proud of him, even if I tried. And now I'm left to speculate if he ever knew this.

Somehow, I find it my responsibility to console Scott's dad. With his mom, there's such a large knife wedged between us, but with Mr. Parrish, it may be easier since he's an older version of Scott.

It makes my heart physically hurt. The idea of thinking of Scott as a mature man, in his early forties—a couple of kids calling him dad. It's with all the what-ifs I know this will never happen, I fall to my knees, a sobbing scream escaping my mouth. Now, both the father and wife are in a grief-stricken state, our actions and erratic movements unable to be understood by anyone unless they've been through this.

Scott's dad wanted him—us—to move to California.

He'd begged Scott, who only ever wanted to work to restore old cars and trucks. His dad offered him a job at his company. Scott had been equally skilled in woodworking. Maguire wanted Scott to come work for him with a chance to go in as partners in a restoration shop for older vehicles, eventually. But, when Christine found this out, she'd flown off the handle, screaming and accusing Scott of loving Maguire more than her.

In Scott's own mind, if he chose a neutral ground, he'd not hurt his mother. The military offered him a way of caring for me. He was working toward a goal. A family was part of our plan, but in his own way, he wouldn't have to choose his mom over his dad. He didn't blame his father. He understood where the selfishness lay. And maybe that's why seeing Christine's face in pain and mourning is too much to take. If she'd just let Scott have his desire, working with his dad, he'd still be alive.

In one part of the room, crying, I'm aware of strong arms consoling me. For a second, a brief second only, I almost believe they are Scott's. Hell, his dad has his same exact touch, and when he begins to speak, I swear it's Scott. "Shh, darlin'." Although Scott would call me Holly. "It's going to be okay, Holland." Shit, *Holland* sounds just like my husband would have said it to me, as he'd stroke my brown hair, stopping at the purple ends, always fixating on them.

And Maguire is doing the same thing. The purple ends of my hair are in my face. I'm left to remember how they had been this color since I'd been with Scott. At that time, it had been all purple. Before, no one ever knew what color of the rainbow would grace my head. But he was partial to purple on me and purple is what it stayed since he asked me out all those years ago. Though, now I only dye the ends of my hair this color.

"Mr. Parrish." My words are barely audible to me. But I don't want to open my eyes that somehow are closed, and in them, I can imagine it's Scott, my husband, my soul mate holding me. But as soon as I think it, I back away.

"Oh, darlin', you don't need to worry about me," his father says. "Scott would want me to make sure you're okay." He's backed up, too and I've forgotten all together my husband is actually in the room with me. I've not had the courage to open the casket yet. I'm not sure I can look at him. I requested his casket to remain closed until I can bring myself to stare at his lifeless body.

I need to breathe and to think, as I work up the nerve to face my husband. "Umm, Mr. Parrish, could you give me a couple minutes with Scott?"

Taking a Kleenex, he wipes his eyes, only for me to look into the exact hazel green eyes of my late husband. He doesn't say a word but walks to the door.

"Wait, Mr. Parrish, Scott made me promise to give you this letter if anything happened to him. He asked you to read it right away." I turn because I'm a bit jealous of this letter. He has final words from Scott when, I, the wife, don't.

He's wiping his eyes, as Scott had when he arrived home from one of his last tours, the same one his close friend was killed in. Carbon copy doesn't quite explain the similarities in them, all the way down to the same pointy nose they share. It's all too eerie.

"Sure, darlin'. And please call me Maguire." He shuts the door behind him and I'm left in the presence of my husband's body.

CHAPTER 3

The envelope reads:
Holly, honey, in case I'm gone—please give this to my dad immediately.

In the years Scott has talked about Holland, at least six years, I've never heard my son call his wife, Holly. It's cute, his own little name just for her. Oh, how I wish I could have known him more.

I saw him four or maybe five times a year. I'd rent a place near him and Chris, taking him for those couple weeks. We'd made furniture together, mostly gifts he'd set aside for Holland and himself. And he'd come home to stay with me for a month, too. But now, twenty-two years of having the honor of being his dad just wasn't enough. It leads me to think of how he'd talked about Holland.

I'm going to marry her one day, Dad. I knew it the first day she'd moved to town and I saw her. When you know, you know.

And I was nothing but jaded, counseling him to exhaustion that young love is hard. I didn't give him the support he needed and fuck, he sure didn't get it from Christine.

My hands tremble as they sweep across the sealed back. These are the last words I'll ever get from Scott. And whether they are spoken or written, the thought is sobering.

My mind wanders for a moment, and I need it to, to anything but this being the last goodbye from my son. In it, I think of Holland. Scott once told me he loved her crazy colors so much because it showed him she didn't give two fucks about what others thought of her.

But the envelope in my hands is a double-edged sword. I want to rip into this letter, absorb it, and have Scott's last words live inside of me forever. But then, when I'm done, he's basically gone. *My son will be forever gone.*

The tears fall from my eyes so quickly I move the letter to avoid ruining it with my waterworks. I pull out a single piece of paper. One last page is all I have of my boy. Before I open the paper that's folded in thirds, I take in a deep breath. I unfold it, carefully, and I'm not surprised by his signature sloppy penmanship. Us lefties are known to have an almost lazy kind of chicken scratch. I laugh at this remembrance. It drove Christine crazy—just one of the many things my son got from me.

His first words still me, and my gaze stays on them. *Dear Dad.* Shit, this will be the last time I'm referred to as Dad. Because Chris made me so jaded, I never tried to find a woman to settle down with. And I'm no longer a dad. Not after today, not after I bury my son.

I stop to let this sink in. I'm a father without a son? Is this possible? My lips tremble at the thought of the last time I'd seen him only a month ago. He never brought Holland, wanting to spend as much time together, just him and me. If I'd known it was all the time I would get with him, would I have held him longer? Done anything different? It doesn't matter, not now that I essentially have my father status stripped from me.

As if staring at *Dear Dad* isn't enough to rip my heart out, I begin to devour the letter and his last words.

Dear Dad,

Fuck, If you're reading this, it means I'm gone. I had one dream, growing old with Holland. Death won't stop me from providing for her, though. And because you're the best man I know, what I'm about to ask you—I know you'll do for me. Please take care of Holland. Take her back to California with you. It's my last request and a lot—I know. But I'm placing my most precious possession in your hands.

See, we don't have much saved and the military won't let Holland stay in government quarters long after my death. I have very little to provide for her if I die. I have my SGLI (life insurance), but it's not enough after she pays for school. But she's talented in design. Please help her get on her feet. Love her like you love me. She has nothing to go back to in Virginia. Her family will suck the little life insurance she has of mine dry.

Mom would have felt so abandoned if I went straight to you from high school. But if I trust anyone with Holland, it's you.

One of my regrets in life is not fighting Mom to come live with you. By the time I knew I could stand up to her, I had met Holland. Please don't tell Mom this. She tried; I know she did. She loves me, this I never doubted. But I wish I knew you better, Dad.

Please know that every moment we had together, I treasured. I know that's not a real dude-like thing to say, but

I did. You made me the man who Holland fell in love with. Let her know when she falls in love again, it's okay! I want everything for her that we couldn't have together.

And, Dad, I know Mom did you wrong. You never made me choose, but it made you cynical. That's why you've never committed to anyone else. Please, find a woman you love and live the life I couldn't.

You will always be a dad—my dad.

Love,

Scott

He has given me closure and purpose. In his honor, I'll make sure Holland is taken care of.

The casket has remained closed and I'm almost positive I'll crumble if I'm to look at the man I've planned my whole life around. With my hand on the vessel my soul mate will be lowered into the ground inside, a sheen of sweat covers me. I've not been able to do this on my own, but that's what I am—on my own.

I've already been visited by the Army housing officer, explaining I have thirty days to vacate the property. I've known this, Scott isn't the only person to die in action. They certainly take no time kicking the spouse out who has lost their forever. My forever was killed for this country and I'll soon be homeless. Sure, I have a life insurance allotment, but it will be meant solely to get me through school and help with my immediate needs.

Going home is my only option, for now, but Scott

never wanted this for me, crawling back to my parents, to a home where their neglect made me the girl Scott had to rebuild. My hand is still on the casket.

"We had so many dreams, baby. This was never part of our plan."

My fingers retract, I want to claw something, hurt someone. Hatred spurns through me for many reasons and I wonder if being pissed at my dead husband is right. Of course, my emotions are so raw—I'm in uncharted waters I'd never waded in before. I'm mad at Scott for leaving me.

I'm not sure you can put a name on what my parents did. They never physically abused me. Neglect is what it was. Sure, I had three meals a day and clothes on my back. A roof over my head was never in question. But I was left to my own accords from an early age, to work as they commanded. We never talked. I was just there. I'd speculated that they never wanted children, yet, here I am. They'd never tucked me into bed or read me a story. My parents were absent for every basketball game I'd participated in, even when we'd made it to state. I could go weeks without talking to them. And through this, they made sure to pay for every activity I was in and bought me my most valued possession, my sewing machine. But that stuff really didn't matter, not when I was a ghost—and I still am. Even when Christine called them to tell them their son-in-law died, they sent me a text, telling me I had a place to come if I needed them.

They're six hours away and do not have the respect to attend my husband's funeral. And of course, Christine offers her house, too, only because she loved Scott so much. She hates me and taking her up on her offer would be hell in itself. Both choices are awful.

Though I'd have Scott's SGLI from the service, it

would only stretch so far, and it's a lengthy process. His money will put me through school and will be the sole purpose of it.

"Ah, Scott."

My hand slides down the casket as it had when it slipped down his body when we made love. He was a tender lover, putting my needs before his. But that's what he did in our life. He wanted to get me out of the clutches of my parents. He didn't want to disappoint his mom by moving to California to work with his father. He did the only other thing he could think of to prove to me he was always on my side—Team Holland all the way. It's what he used to say. He had joined the Army so we could marry, with the ability to provide for me.

I lower my head to the box containing his body, to where I believe his face is. "How do I do this on my own, Scott? Where do I even begin?"

I'm not talking about a job or money. I'm resourceful, I'll figure it out, but loneliness will consume me, without the anticipation of Scott walking in the door. Tears fall on the beauty of the wood that holds my best friend, or his remains, I should say, when I swear his large muscular arms surround me—and I break. Every fiber of my being holds onto him because now that I have him back, I'll never let go. Then I turn, only to see it's not my husband. It's my father-in-law.

CHAPTER 4

Maguire

S he's still in shock when I pull into the drive of the house Scott and Holland shared together. It may be military housing, but I can see in detail the effort Scott had taken to make his home stand out among the other units. The concrete carport is immaculate, not one ounce of clutter compared to the other houses in the cul-de-sac. The gutters are not overflowing with leaves and shit like their neighbors, although the grass has turned a little brown due to the weather, it's trimmed neatly. Even the windowsills and shutters look tidily painted compared to the chipped paint on their neighbors' houses.

He didn't get this little bit of work ethic from Christine. Oh, fuck no. Every six months, when I'd rent a cabin for Scott and me to bond, she'd talk me into a day's worth of chores. It was our little silent agreement. I'd complete her honey-do list, and she'd leave us alone for the entire time I was with him. *"Let Scott help you, might as well show him how to do some of this shit, it's not like he's learning it from you on the other side of the country."*

Though he had because he worked in my factory for the summers in California.

The truth was, Christine thought I should pack up my life and follow them. And I would have done it, but she became more demanding with child support each year. I couldn't afford to start over and Parrish & Landon Custom Furniture had been picking up. Every year, I thought I could start up a factory in Virginia and I'd come back from a month of being inundated by all things Christine and I never took the leap. Scott had been the one who suffered because of it.

I know Chris is hurting and part of me still loves the woman who gave me Scott for twenty-two years but hell, I can't help but hate her, too.

I rummage for the keys to the house as Holland sits next to me in the truck Scott and I refurbished together, in almost a catatonic state. "Hold on, darlin'." Opening the door for her and pulling her out, she's as light as a feather. I'm able to turn the knob to the door and kick it lightly open at the same time with Holland in my arms.

Walking over the threshold of their house, I'm assaulted by everything Scott. It's overwhelming— everything that was him. There's a North Carolina Tarheels blanket strewn across the couch. A picture of some of his buddies from my factory is hung up on the adjacent wall from the door. His leather bomber jacket I'd bought for him a couple Christmases ago is on the coat rack. This all feels too surreal—like an out of body experience.

I follow the hallway back to where I believe the bedrooms are and deposit Holland on her bed. On one of the end tables is their wedding picture, the same one that's on my desk at home. They got married at the justice of the peace, but it doesn't mean the smile on Scott's face isn't anything but happiness. And next to the picture is a small cast iron trinket of a John Deere tractor. Every time I saw him or sent him a present, I'd drive down to this little custom toy store and pick up the newest item. When he'd turned thirteen, I'd stopped with the tractors, thinking he was too old for them. When I called him to wish him a happy birthday, I had asked if he liked the new skateboard he'd talked about for months.

"Yeah, Dad, it's perfect." But something in his voice warns the dad in me that there's more.

"Son, did I order the wrong one?" It's possible. After all, I had relied on Christine to give me the right information.

"Oh, no, Dad, sorry! It's great. It's what I wanted." But still he's quiet, and I need to get to the heart of the issue.

"Scott, it's okay. Can you tell me what's bothering you, please?" I hate I'm not there for him, to really see the hurt in his eyes that radiates in his voice through the phone.

"Oh, it's nothing, really," Scott hems and haws with me and I lose my patience.

My tone is a little stronger this time, and he has to know I'm not playing around. "Scott Jameson Parrish, just tell me. I can't help you if you don't get it off your chest."

"Man, Dad, I'll sound selfish complaining about it." When I don't say a word, he continues, "I love the tractors you get me. Every time I see them, it makes me think of you and me. It's our thing, and when I didn't get one, I thought this part was over for us."

It's then, I understand our bond is stronger than the many fucking states that separate us. And he still longs for it—the connection we share, in the form of small five-dollar tractors. Age be damned, he'd get them.

A small laugh falls from my mouth and I let out a sigh

of relief. *"Son, this is something I can fix. Truth be told, I was a little sad, not going in our shop to buy one for you. I assumed you were getting too old for them and shit, I'm glad you're not."*

He returns the sentiment right away, "Thanks, Dad, for understanding."

I'm standing at the foot of the bed, taking in the little toy that meant so much to him and fuck, until now, I had no idea how much they meant to me, too.

I'm in bed, not even sure how I got here. All I know is I wake to the worst nightmare. The lamp light is on and I smell eggs. Scott must be cooking for me. I'm assuming it's ham and cheese omelets in the skillet. I know it's this because Scott can't cook anything else if his life depends on it. Not that I'm a great cook either. But none of this registers when I fling myself out of bed, I undress, ready to surprise my husband. After the humdinger of the dream, I'm going to blow his mind and do it very well.

"Hey, babe." My seductive low vibrato rings through. Scott knows what I sound like when I'm ready to be taken in any part of the house. "You won't believe the awful freakin' dream I had."

Turning the corner, it's not Scott standing in the kitchen ready to flip the omelets, it's his dad. As he twists around, seeing me in nothing but my birthday suit, it all comes back to me. It's not a blip on the radar that I'm without clothes and I pool to the floor.

"Oh, hell, it's true. It's true. It isn't a nightmare."

From my vantage point, Maguire leaves the kitchen quickly. In a split second, his feet rush for me, and something covers my body. The warmth of the blanket reminds me that Scott is this man's son, and he's lost as much as I have, if not more. Clinging to the blanket, I try to stand, only to stumble. But I find my way back to my room, mine and Scott's. Through my tears and cries, I can just hear it between my own sobs. But if I stop enough to listen, down the hallway, I can hear the accompanying cries of Scott's dad for the man we both loved and miss.

The funeral came and went and my parents never showed up. They weren't there for me as a child, why did I expect different as an adult? Though my mom texted me, asking me to come home. She probably googled that the SGLI is a couple hundred thousand dollars. Where it sounds like a lot, it's not. It'll be just enough to get by with my immediate life.

As much as I don't want to, Christine's offer is the best. Even with her manipulation, she won't have any intention of getting her hands on Scott's life insurance. She has enough love and respect for her son than to try anything along these lines. Living with her until I can make arrangements will be its own little hell.

Still a week after the funeral, Maguire is in town, coming to check on me daily. Today is no different. He's a good man, the one reason Scott didn't turn into his mom. But being around him is too hard, because this man, my father-in-law, is the spitting image of my husband.

He's made himself comfortable in my house, making coffee, cooking dinners, and doing any upkeep that Scott typically did when he was home.

"Mr. Parrish," I say when he appears in the carport, shirtless, after working on Scott's truck, "I appreciate your help." This man shows me the goods I'm going to miss in my own man. "Hey, could we talk for a second?" He plans to stay another week in the motel up the road to help me pack.

"Oh, yeah, darlin', I needed to chat with you, too. I got grease on my shirt; do you mind if I grab one of Scott's?"

I can't help but laugh. Where Scott was big, I'm almost positive, he was still filling out. Both men are long, a runners body, but Maguire is certainly a full-size man. Like Scott, he towers over me at about 6' 3". As he turns from me, I notice a small tattoo on his chest right over his heart, but I can't make it out.

"Something funny?" he asks.

It's one of the few times I've seen him smile. It's handsomely hot.

How do I put this delicately? "Well, you're welcome to them. But I don't think they'll fit you comfortably."

Stretching his hands over his head, his smile never falters. "You calling this old man fat?"

I would never call Maguire Parrish fat in his forty-year-old body. No, it makes me ache to know what Scott could have matured into if he'd lived. "I'm not saying that. It's just Scott was not as big as you, but his clothes are kept in the spare room to the right, in the closet. Help yourself."

I start coffee for him. The man loves that sludge. The shower starts, and I wonder how much Scott indeed looks like his father, deep down. I flush at this idea and giggle because I miss my husband so much.

I'm standing at the window overlooking our cul-de-sac when Maguire's unexpected words startle me. "Yeah, darlin'.'" He's towel drying his hair, appearing in the kitchen as I pour his coffee and steep my tea. "I guess you're right, this man is fat," he says.

Turning toward him, every muscle is revealed through Scott's simple blue shirt. I get more of a bird's-eye view of his body now than I did when he was shirtless and nothing is left to the imagination.

"Ah, you read my mind, darlin'." Even the way he says darlin' has me seeing my father-in-law in a different light. I need him to stop, but it's part of his personality. "Let's enjoy our drinks in the sun."

I follow him to the covered patio and it's then a tear escapes my eye. I'm going to miss this place. It had been ours together—mine and Scott's—and when I say goodbye to this little home, it's one of the last pieces I'll have of him. Of *us*.

"I'm going to head to the motel after this to get a shirt that doesn't look like it is part of my skin," he begins. "Then scrounge up some boxes so we can pack. Have you given any thought to what you're going to do?"

"Um, my only option until Scott's SGLI comes in, is to move in with Christine." My own body shudders in pain at this idea when Maguire places his coffee on the table between us, his elbows on his knees.

"I wanted to wait until we got through the funeral, but you know that letter you gave me from Scott?" he asks and I'd almost forgotten. I nod my head in anticipation of Scott's last words to his father. "He wanted me to take you home. I have an apartment over my garage that I use as my workspace. We could incorporate your design ideas, especially in our décor branch of the company. I've spoken with Ned and Diane, who runs the design division. We can work around your school hours. And quite honestly,

Holland, it's the last thing my son asked of me, so I want to honor his wishes."

The words don't permeate my mind. First, they only float around me. Of course, Scott would come up with a backup plan, someone to watch over me. I'm not sure why I'm surprised.

CHAPTER 5

"This is a fucking mistake." "Christine, in her Christine way, is causing a scene while the women's shelter and local Red Cross chapter are taking items Holland can't keep—along with all of Scott's clothes.

Holland's head whips back to the loud melodrama of her mother-in-law.

"Keep your voice down, Chris!" I shout, bringing me into her commotion. "It's the last thing our son asked of me, of course, I'm going to honor his wishes."

"Let me do it. Let me help Holland. It's not appropriate for you to care for her—anyway with me, she's near her parents."

I laugh but not in the ha-ha kind of way. "You mean the parents that are six hours away and couldn't come to their son-in-law's funeral?" She shrugs her reply, but I'm not done. "Plus, Chris, you aren't the easiest person to get along with. You don't even like her." My voice becomes almost a whisper, Holland's eyes catching my own every so often. "Anyway, her skill set is suited for a great job I can provide.

And I built that apartment above my workspace. It was meant for Scott when he was old enough to live his life as an adult." I never have blamed her for being her—the needy bitch she is—and this is the closest I've ever come to actually accusing her of pushing our son into the service when he wanted to move Holland and himself to California. "And furthermore, he always planned to move back to Cali, so he wants this for his wife." I walk away, leaving her speechless. I'm unable to console her or offer anything else. She's taken so much from me—I'm finished.

"The only things I want besides the sewing machine he'd bought for me to replace the one my parents gave me years ago, is the table and chairs you two made for my wedding gift and his truck." And with that, I knew we'd be taking the cross-country trip in his old 1951 Chevrolet pickup truck we worked on every time I visited.

It's a beauty, an almost yellow gold. Scott had loved the year and model of this truck. "I can't part with it. I know it would be more logical to keep my car, but I need to hold onto this. It's a part of him. I'll feel as if he's with me in the passenger seat, grabbing my knee." A smile forms on her face and in it, I imagine her envisioning this scene in her mind. "He'll be criticizing my driving as he always does." It's not a dig but a fond fact she finds amusing when her lips turn upward. "Fiddlesticks, he hated riding with me. And what always surprised me was he was a scary driver in his own right."

I nod, now with a grin at all the close calls we'd had over the years since he'd started driving. "Yeah, you're sure as shit right about that." Though she's correct about having a reliable vehicle, if she hadn't held on to his truck, I sure as hell would have. "We'll ship the table with the rest of your stuff." The military is taking care of this. "And I'll go get some tarps for all the luggage. There's not much room up front for your sewing machine, but I'll make sure it's safe."

She nods, and with my declaration, protecting the last thing my son bought for her, she believes me at face value.

Looking around the rest of their house, the walls are bare, the furniture is mostly gone, and she's given away more crap than she'll care to admit.

"I'll put you up for the night. And we can head out tomorrow."

I've seen the way she reacted in the last couple of days as her friends came to say goodbye. Everyone loved Scott, this isn't a surprise, not because I was his dad. He was a good guy and funny as hell. If I have to see her tear up one more time at any more of her farewells as she calls them, I think I very well may hit something. It's all tearing me up inside.

It's a hard thing to grieve alongside someone you don't know very well, yet with the love that we both share for Scott, it's easy when it comes to Holland. Even with Christine, Holland is kind. The girl will give anyone the shirt off her back. And after she's lost so much already, she's now losing another part of her life—her friends who were, in essence, her family.

"Um, Mr. Parrish, I can't do that. I have the air mattress and…"

Rubbing my forehead, I internally moan at the formality she shows me, after me asking her over and over again to call me Maguire. "Holland." My tone is a little harsher coming out as a warning and she stiffens, but then she laughs. "Okay, I'll bite, what's so funny?" I ask.

"Shitake mushrooms, I'm sorry. But you sound so much like Scott. When I pushed him, or he was irritated enough with me, his tone would lower, like yours. Sometimes he'd force a laugh. Even down to the emphasis with part of my name." She's now giggling hysterically and I'm not sure if it's funny or it's just the first time she's not crying at the thought of Scott that has her showing this kind of emotion. "I'm sorry, Mr. Parrish, I couldn't help it." She offers no further explanation, but it's nice to see her smile. It looks good on her.

"Okay, glad I could put a grin on your sweet face." These words are delivered more seductively, the pitch of my voice is one I'd typically reserved for sweet talking a lady into my bed for the night. She has picked up on it. Hell, maybe Scott did the same thing with her and we both turn red.

I skip over this awkward as fuck weirdness when I decide to ask, "Do you not swear? I mean, I don't want to offend you."

She smirks, moving her eyes downward like I've embarrassed her. "Um, no, you won't offend me. I mean, I do curse, when it's warranted—believe me. I wait, especially with Scott, so he could really gauge my anger."

I don't say this, but I know for some reason, hearing this beauty swear would seem unnatural.

"About the hotel, we can get an earlier move on tomorrow. It's no biggie, and if it makes you feel better, you can pay me back." Though, I don't have any intention of accepting her money.

"Oh, poop on a stick," she declares out of nowhere.

There's this light bulb moment on her face. "You bring up a good point. I'm strapped until the life insurance is released. So, please keep a record of the gas and hotels and meals. You're not footing the bill due in part to me not letting go of Scott's truck. So, I intend to pay you back, every penny."

I nod my head. No reason to piss off the girl who I'll be sharing the next five days with over this subject. Again, she's crazy if she thinks I'll take one cent from Scott's insurance.

Her gaze falls to the floor. She can't look at me and I wonder what all of this is about. I'm close to challenging her, to make her tell me when I stop. I give her the couple seconds she needs to voice an apparent concern. She finally begins, "Christine told me she thinks I'm using you as a meal ticket. Never mind the fact this had always been our plan, moving to California after he was released from the service."

Fucking Christine. See, I want to help her. Shit, she lost her son, just as I have but it doesn't mean for one second, I'll allow her to fuck with Holland. Scott asked me to care for her, and it's what I'll do if I have to run interference on Holland's part with her psycho mother-in-law, I'll gladly do this. It's not like it's any different than the shit Christine has been pulling my whole adult life.

Holland

I'm settled into my room, the one Maguire insisted on paying for. I hate this, being indebted to my father-in-law. Yet, at the same time, it's Scott's way of taking care of me. The second Maguire suggested it, the mixed feelings of such an offer washed through me like water and oil, neither one mixing well together.

Living with Maguire will be the ultimate punishment. Everything he does reminds me of Scott. From the way he changes the oil to wiping his mouth after each bite of food, to washing his hands—and so much more. This is the older version of my husband in front of me.

Next, is the fact that Maguire is at the top of the most handsome *men on earth* list. His ruggedness, the way he changed the tires on the truck last week, to how he pours himself a cup of coffee, or how he puts Christine in her place, which I secretly love, have him elevated to a new level in my book.

This in and of itself, makes me feel ashamed. Ashamed that Maguire's very nature sets my soul on fire. Is it that Maguire is my husband in an older man's body that has me craving his touch, a sample of the goods if you will? Shame engulfs me at this idea. *Did I really just contemplate this?* My husband's body isn't even cold in the grave and I'm ready to find a replacement? No, this can't be—the love I have for Scott transcends time and place.

"Get it together, Holland," I order myself, catapulting from the bed, burning a hole in the carpet as I pace back and forth. "This is a bad idea, and horribly tempting." I continue to speak to myself as if Scott is in front of me. "No, but it's only a bad idea if…" Yes! That's the answer to my prayers. It's only a bad idea when two consent. I won't be consenting; I have enough self-restraint. I have a lot more self-respect than to hop into bed with my father-in-law. Plus, Maguire does, too. And after all, this is what my husband wanted. I'll take the job, take the apartment until I can find something in town I can afford, and we'd see each other as a family does, at holidays.

Looking at myself in the mirror, I say, "Good plan,

Holland." I almost believe it myself.

CHAPTER 6

"Don't we have GPS?" Maguire scoffs at my obvious statement. I'm sitting on the small desk behind him at the rinky-dink complementary office space he's planning our cross-country trip in. He's printing map upon map, not to mention, the fifty-state atlas he bought this morning before the sun was up at the closest Walmart.

"GPS really should serve as a guide, darlin'." He switches between calling me darlin' like I'm a long-distance niece he sees every couple of decades to just Holland. He seems pained when he uses both in my vicinity—like my name is the forever reminder of Scott. "You never know if it picks up alternate routes and we've got to be prepared for every situation." He turns in the swivel chair. A crew neck shirt is so tight around his biceps that I wonder if it will rip and expose his bare skin. "Anyway, I'm pretty confident in Scott's truck—worked on it myself but, hell, we want to be safe."

For some reason, being with Maguire, I'm as safe as

when I was in Scott's strong arms — no one could get to me then, and no one can get to me now. I roll my eyes, pushing myself off the desk. My skirt gets caught in the chair I have been sitting on. "Well, shit," I state the obvious. He must have seen my cheetah print undies Scott loved so much on me. He turns his head quickly out of respect. First, he'd seen me in my birthday suit, now in my skimpy leopard thong. This is adding up for a great start to our trip.

I find it hard to speak at first, with a heated flush covering my face. "Me and my embarrassed ass are going to wait for you outside in the truck while you micromanage our trip."

We're running to this little diner up the road he has had most of his meals at for the past couple weeks, for dinner, then back to the hotel for an early night.

"Hey, Holland," he calls, and I can still feel my cheeks burning, which must now look like strawberries. "Has anyone ever called you a smart ass?" he deadpans.

"Hell yes, all the time and guess what? You get my smart-ass-ness for three-thousand miles." I turn to take my leave; happy he sees a little bit more of me. And, after my panty exposure, hell, he's certainly seen a little bit more than I'd wanted.

The next morning greets me. I'm a mixture of nerves with an emotion of the unknown washing through me. When my eyes see the text, I'm already in tears saying goodbye to the life I led with Scott.

Sarah: Honey, Mark got home last night. We're meeting you at the hotel before you leave. We can't let you go without hugging you.

I laugh at this girl who's become my sister. My heart lurches at all I'll miss. The curtains I've been trying to make for their little girl is still just fabric I packed away in the hopes of finishing before her baby arrives in this world. I had planned to be there for the birth. I've taken birthing classes with her, in case Mark wasn't home in time.

Mark has been Scott's best friend from the moment they met in boot camp. It's funny how friendship is sped up in the military. These people become your family fast.

Hopping up out of bed, I take the quickest of showers. Afterward, I get dressed, grabbing a pair of unicorn leggings and a long neon green top, which is about two sizes too big. But it's comfortable, and for the next five days in Scott's truck, it's what I crave.

Not a second too soon, there's a little knock on the door after I brush my teeth. Opening it quickly, there stands Mark and Sarah—our dearest friends. I don't get a hello out before she and her huge belly envelop me in a hug. She's already crying. Bringing my head up, there are tears in Mark's eyes, too.

Mark couldn't get back in time for the funeral. Typically, they'd not send him home at all, even with Sarah only four weeks from delivering. But when Scott was killed, Mark was injured—sent to Germany for rehab.

Sarah finally lets go of me, and I melt into the arms of my husband's best friend. "Fuck, Holly! I'm so sorry." Besides Scott, there's no one else in the world that calls me Holly except Mark. "I couldn't save him. I tried, please know I tried."

Sarah, who's now sitting on the bed, is crying uncontrollably. When she found out Mark was with Scott the moment he was killed, she'd told me after the funeral how guilty she felt that her husband was spared.

Cupping his face, I make him look at me. "No, Mark, it's not your fault, not ever. And Scott wouldn't want you to blame yourself." I go to hug him again, to be his comfort. But as I do, he's yanked from me, and being pushed into the outside wall adjacent from my room. When I look at the strong arms that are about to tear him apart, I see Maguire.

Hands are roving all around Holland's body. It's all that I'm able to take in before I have the man that's obviously forcing himself on her against the wall on the outside of the motel.

"What the fuck are you doing to my daughter-in-law?"

The kid, no older than Scott, pushes off of me. "Calm the fuck down, old man," he chimes and I'm about to hit him until I recognize him.

"Old man? Huh."

The boy I'm about to pummel puts his arms out and hugs me. "Shit, Maguire, for an old man, you're strong as fuck."

I turn to Holland, her hands on her hips. She's not amused by all the commotion. "Mark, sorry, son," I say, and I realize that Mark—Scott's best friend is just another reminder of what I've lost.

This time, he brings me in for a hug, not just a greeting but one that encompasses both our grief. "Maguire, shit, it could have been me. One foot over was the difference in where we were standing. Scott should be with you right now."

I've never met Mark's wife, but she appears behind

LIKE *Father* LIKE *Son*

him, carrying a watermelon in her stomach. Reaching her hand out, I don't shake it. I hug her as if she's family and she is. "I'm so sorry for your loss," she adds, tears in her own eyes. The words her husband has spoken had to have wounded her. Fate if you will, it's a fickle bastard—the difference between life and death was a fucking foot.

Mark had flown out with Scott after his technical school, and this kid in front of me stole a piece of my heart. He doesn't have a dad, and Scott felt he needed some sort of father figure in his life, and we bonded, quickly. As dedicated to the service and his wife as Scott had been to the Army and Holland, it was easy to care for this kid.

"Sorry I took a swing at you. I saw Holland crying and just reacted."

He wipes a tear from his face and swings his arm around his wife. "It's what Scott wanted—for you to watch out for Holly, to make sure she's okay. And I knew there was no one better."

We begin to say our goodbyes, and I'm hauling Holland's luggage downstairs to the truck.

Looking over at her as I put the truck in drive, large tears free flow down her cheeks. "Holland, I can't tell you it's going to get better. I'm not sure it ever will. I miss him so much, but I can promise that I'll take care of you and make sure you have all you need in this life."

She reaches for my hand and squeezes it. "I know you will, Mr. Parrish. I know you will." The smile on her face may be what I need to get me through the years without my son in my life.

"It's pretty much a straight shot," I say, her eyes staring out the window as it did when we left the hotel right off base from Camp Lejeune.

"Hmm?" she asks, not moving her head.

"The interstate, pretty much straight freeway," I add.

"Um, okay." Bending over, she grabs a pillow—and positions it against the window.

"Hey, you can't go to sleep on me now," I tease, finally getting her to look over at me.

The girl and her outfits crack me up. I guess she has on a pair of yoga pants. That's what Kat says they are called. It's not like Kat ever gets dressed up to come to my house. Hell, she barely even stays after she sucks my cock and I've filled her up. It's a mutually beneficial arrangement that I guess will have to continue at her house after Holland moves in.

Along with her yoga pants that are bright pink and have unicorns on them, mind you, is a bright neon green t-shirt that covers her ass. Shit, can I say ass when it comes to my daughter-in-law? This girl has me all jumbled up inside and I can't explain why. I fuck women, not girls who have come into womanhood two seconds ago.

"I'm sorry, Maguire. You're right, it's not fair to ask you to do all the heavy lifting on this trip."

"Oh, darlin', it's not that," I say, shifting down into fourth gear as I take the exit for the gas station. "I can't stand to see that pretty face of yours with any more tears." Shit, did I just flirt with Holland?

She closes her eyes, turning her head away from me but the blush creeping onto her face is so fucking adorable.

"We need gas again?" she asks, taking out that fucking notepad and pen to write down the amount I'm paying on gas and snacks.

"Yep, though it certainly doesn't get the gas mileage

of a new truck, it's not doing too bad. I won't let it get below half a tank."

Moving her full lips into something I've barely seen on her face in the past couple of weeks, she smiles. "Hell, you and Scott are so much alike."

I love the memories she paints for me when it comes to Scott. It's a punch to the gut sometimes when I have to remind myself he's gone. But shit, the memories are all I have now. And whenever she points out the similarities, I know I had an impact on my son's life.

She turns from me like she said something wrong. Grabbing for her hand, I pull at it until she turns her head. "Darlin', please don't ever stop talking about Scott. It's how I can get through this. Remembering him, knowing I had a bearing on the man he was. I never thought I did enough for him. But shit, when you are around, reminding me, I almost believe it."

Another tear escapes her eye. "I just miss him so much, Maguire." She turns as if she's about to say more, but she stops. At least she's not calling me Mr. Parrish anymore.

"Having you to remind me of the man I raised helps me."

Twisting her head to me, she merely returns, *"Having you to remind me of the great son you raised helps me."*

CHAPTER 7

Maguire

"We didn't get out of the Carolinas today? Fiddlesticks, this trip will take forever." I'd say she's mumbling to herself, but she's rather loud. Actually, her own whisper scares me.

"Yeah, it'll take at least five days. I don't want to push the truck too much. Plus..." What do I say? I don't want to push *her*? She's grieving after all. She needs her rest to take care of herself and hell—*to be taken care of.*

"I'm not some delicate flower. I won't wilt." Her hair is in her eyes but her words, the way she stresses *I won't wilt*, makes her meaning clear. She can claim this all day long, and nothing will stop me from keeping my promise to my son.

"Listen, Miss, I'm just worried about you."

"Miss?"

"Yeah, growing up, my dad called me mister. He'd call my girl cousins miss. I don't think he even cared to learn any of our names." It's not a joke but she laughs anyway, and the air is a little lighter between us. "Come on." I grab her bags before she can pull them from me. "Let's get us some rooms."

She stops in the parking lot and when she doesn't follow me, I fib, just a little as I begin, "Don't worry. I'm taking notes. And you can pay me back when Scott's insurance comes in." Her smile tells me I'm correct—this girl is just not strong, but stubborn as hell.

"Thanks, Mister," she counters, and I laugh—happy that somewhere inside of her she's found something that makes us just a little bit more comfortable with one another.

She doesn't follow me to secure rooms for us. Rounding the corner of the motel office, I find her on the bench in her loud outfit, staring straight ahead.

"Penny for your thoughts?" I ask. She's still a stranger to me yet family at the same time.

"It's silly and I'll seem ungrateful," she replies when she twists her head toward mine. I'm lost in the almost dark chocolate brown of her eyes. They are different than any others I've seen, but as is everything of Holland Parrish, different should really be her first name.

"Oh, I seldom get my feelings hurt, darlin'. Seriously, the little smile on your face, it's nice to see. I've gotta know what put it there."

She scrunches her face together as if she's hiding from me. "Okay, but don't say I didn't warn you." She looks away but her voice carries when she continues, "It's just, you and Scott have this uncanny ability to find the most obscure and sometimes scary motels to call home for the night."

It's now I pick up on her southern accent and it's cute. No, scratch that, it's more than cute, but I shouldn't think these thoughts about my son's wife.

"Ah, yes! You're calling my choice cheap," I begin with a deep chuckle on the verge of escaping my mouth.

"See, I sound like a witch when you say it this way."

She's looking away, and her voice oozes with concern. "No, darlin'. I'm teasing you. But, believe me, Scott and I certainly shared this trait. It drove his mama crazy."

When a loud burst of laughter bolts from her lips, she quickly covers her mouth with her hands as if she's protecting a lifelong pledge with her best friend.

"Now, what's that about?" I poke her side, playfully tickling her.

Her lips are pursed together and she's scratching her head. "Um...it's just—what didn't upset Christine? Sometimes I think me breathing had her ready to take off my head."

A tight smile crawls over my face. I have no doubt this is true with Christine—it had always been her way in life.

"If I'm not being too nosy, what happened with you two? Scott never knew. He said he barely remembered y'all being together."

Now, it's my turn to scratch my own head. I never wanted Scott to find out and I guess he won't. What's the harm in sharing it with Holland? "I never spoke of it and— well—Christine certainly would never tell him."

"Oh," she begins and it's easy to decipher from what I've shared. "Was it just once?" I pause, not ready to answer yet. Speaking of Christine's infidelity is still salt in the wound. It leaves me wondering in all this shit if Christine and I had stayed together, would our son be six feet under?

Pulling at my shoulders with one hand and rubbing my temples, I think of how to begin. "If it was simply one time, I probably could've forgiven her."

"And she punished you, taking Scott away? Right?"

I never could prove this, but it's how I always felt. "I'm not sure how to answer you." I stand because reliving the nightmare I call my marriage to Christine isn't what I want to do just weeks after burying my son. "Hey, you ready to get some dinner? I'm starving and would like to get a good night's sleep. Want to be on the road by five."

"A.M.?" Her voice almost cracks.

"Oh, not a morning person, darlin'?"

Her scowl has me laughing my ass off because like so many things that are Holland, it's cute as hell.

Nine p.m. rolls around and my eyes are heavy. I'm about to welcome sleep when a loud rap at the door wakes me from an almost slumber.

Opening it, I recognize the desk clerk from earlier. "Hey, everything okay?" I question.

"Yeah, sorry to barge in. I saw you and your daughter earlier and y'all looked like a happy family." I'm confused as to why hours later he's sharing this with me. "After my shift, I stopped at the little bar down the street for a beer." I was almost asleep, and this conversation is going nowhere. "Hell, I'm sorry, this is making no sense." The man must be in his late forties and he's fiddling with his jacket as he speaks. "Your daughter is down at the bar. I don't mean to get in the way, but there are some unruly drifters who…" He hasn't finished his sentence when I grab the truck keys and rush past him.

"Thanks, man," I call back. Hurrying to the truck, it's not long before I'm in front of the little hole in the wall tavern. Pulling open the door, I hear "Cotton Eye Joe" blaring. Man, I hate country music, and on top of this, I'll need a tetanus shot after I leave.

Holland isn't hard to miss. She's in a pair of the

shortest shorts I've ever seen and I'm surprised her ass isn't hanging out. When I get closer, I'm wrong on my first assessment and force my eyes away from that part of my daughter-in-law's body. She's on the stage, dancing in a pair of cowboy boots and three reasonably large men are cheering her on.

I weave through the men, hopping up on the stage to grab my son's wife. "Ah, look who it is. It's my daddy-in-law." Her voice, even louder if it's possible, is also slurred.

"Yo, bro, what are you doing?" This question comes from one of the men watching when Holland leans into me and I can't miss the smell of lilacs that permeate my nose.

"Um, bro," I begin. "I'm taking her back to where we are staying for the night."

Holland is light, and I sling her over my shoulder.

One of the men stops me, his hand on my chest. "Um, I think that's up to the little lady to decide," the biggest of the bros says.

I ball my hands into fists but even in my best day, I could never take on three men at once. Diplomacy needs to be the path I take here, for now anyway. Releasing a cleansing breath, I begin, "So, bro, listen and listen well. This woman just buried her husband."

They don't back off and Holland's rambling is making things worse.

"Ah, don't be a stick in the mud, daddy-in-law, let me play for a while," she whines. Oh, yeah, these men want to play, that's for sure but only over my dead body.

"You heard the lady," one of the other men reply.

"Okay, so you didn't hear me, her husband was killed in action. You want to really do what you have planned to someone's wife who served this country?"

Shaking their heads, all three back up, their hands up

in surrender.

"Um, no, bro, even we understand clear lines." The biggest of the men turn to Holland. "Sorry, ma'am, the man has a point."

I have Holland in Scott's truck and back to the room quickly. I sleep sitting up in the chair near the door, keeping watch over my son's wife, fucking sure as hell I'll keep my very last promise to him.

"Where the hell am I?" I ask in a whisper, my throat feels like sandpaper and a wastebasket is near me. Through the light from the little crack between the curtains, I find I'm faced with the older version of Scott. And as I am almost every day when I wake, I'm reminded he's gone.

His father is taking up the entire stiff chair in front of the door. His neck is in a position no neck should ever be in. He's never changed from yesterday, his boots still on his feet. The gray of his beard really stands out from the ray of sunshine flooding the room. And like I do every time I look heavy at the man who's my father-in-law, I'm reminded of the life I won't ever have with Scott.

But it's more. Sure, Maguire reminds me so much of Scott, but he's also his own man. The pain in his face as he relived the infidelity of Christine haunts me. It's like the pain is still present and as Scott had always speculated, the reason his dad never settled down.

An arm stretching in the air captures my attention when the other hand goes to scrub over his way past five o'clock shadow. Attempting to move his neck, he groans and honestly, I don't blame him. For some reason, I can look at him all day long, though I have to dispel the belief he's my father-in-law. The way I look at him in this light right now isn't father-in-law like at all.

The question still remains, how in the world did I get back to the hotel room. I was at the bar one moment, and the next, I'm in this bed. I try to move as Maguire changes positions, but my head is as heavy as bricks. Fudge nuggets, not only my head but my whole body. Running my hands down my frame, I realize I'm in shorts. They're my booty shorts I'd tease Scott with when I was playing striptease. It was one of our favorite outfits and games. Poop on a stick, what did I do last night? These shorts show most of my ass. And were meant for Scott and Scott alone.

"Morning, darlin'," he begins, but it's not the playful tone I've come to expect from Maguire. "Or should I say, party animal?"

Ah, shoot, it's all coming back to me now. Shoot, shoot, shoot. The fog is lifting little by little and I'm embarrassed as I think of anyone, especially my father-in-law seeing me in my *too* short Daisy Dukes. And it hits me, I called him daddy-in-law the whole time. I have this need to flee, to create as much space between Maguire and myself—as possible.

"Are you reliving last night?" His tone is curt, too curt. Short and annoyed, speaking in this one quick sentence.

"Um, it's all coming back to me." I try to sit up and my stomach begins to curdle. I'm out of bed, running to the bathroom. I don't quite make it to the toilet. The small wastebasket is nothing for what's coming up now. I must puke until it's just stomach acid when a knock on the door lets me know I still have a babysitter in the room.

"Holland, I assume the bar is closed, so I don't have

to worry about you going back." Ah, now he's a dick. I loved my husband without question, but here's a little similarity, too. When Scott would get upset, his dickishness came out in rare form, as is Maguire's right now. "So, you have an hour. We're already three hours behind schedule, and I got shit for sleep."

I push out of the bathroom, him standing at the door, barely letting me out. "I'm not going back to the fucking bar, Maguire," I begin. I hardly swear and it surprises me, too, when it escapes my mouth. It's how I know I'm pissed as hell.

He laughs at me. The asshole *is actually laughing at me.*

"Um, darlin', that word isn't made to form on your lips. I don't like you saying it."

"Well, too fucking bad." I push past him and fall to the bed.

"Holland." His voice is stern like I'm his child.

"Maguire," I retort.

"An hour," he says, now at my door.

"No, there's no way in hell I can travel. Checkout isn't until noon. Let me sleep for three more hours. Please?" I almost beg but I'm a grown ass adult and shit, I don't need his permission.

"We're leaving, we have a schedule to adhere to."

Adhere to. Who the hell speaks like this? "Well, you know, adhere to this." My voice raises a decibel or two and I flip him off.

"Act like a child, I'll treat you like one."

I'm off the bed, so quickly I hold onto the wall to make my way toward him. "Well, excuse me for taking one night to try to forget this shit, my best friend, lover, and the man who was supposed to give me babies is gone forever.

So I got drunk and made some bad choices. Okay, it was a shitty thing to do, I get it. But don't *fucking* treat me like a baby because I'm more than sifting through adult shit right now." I fall back onto the bed, and though it's not the side I slept in last night, it's where I stay.

"Okay, you win, Holland. But I want to be on the road by eleven-thirty, no later, you got it?"

"Yeah, I got it, Sarge," I add, saluting him because I'm a smart ass and I want to piss him off as much as he's pissed me off.

"And, can I trust you'll stay put?"

"I can't even move, and what's funny, I barely drank last night," I add because this is the worst hangover I've ever had for maybe three rum and Cokes.

"Yeah, nice try. No one pukes that much from a couple drinks."

He leaves and I find myself mad at him, scratch that, fucking furious as hell at him, I also find myself equally pissed off at my late husband.

"Man, Scott, " I call out loud. "Your dad sure can be a dick. " It's the last thing I remember.

He's pounding, yes pounding on the door and my eyes must have been glued shut. Dragging my sorry butt out of bed, I pass the mirror and see my hair is sticking up on end. Well, hell, even my hair is hungover.

He's in front of me, a disapproving look on his face the second the open door reveals I'm not close to being ready.

"I said eleven-thirty, Holland." His dick-like tone is still evident. His pitch drops an octave or two and the hazel green of his eyes turn an almost brown.

"I know, Sarge, and I'm sorry. Give me ten minutes to hop in the shower. Do we need gas? I'll be ready when you get back?"

He barges in. "Already got gas. You better take the quickest shower known to mankind."

Hell, he's gone from a dick to a prick. When I told Scott once there were levels to his dickish ways, I explained prick was worse than dick. And that's where his dad is right now.

I fall back onto the bed, my head in my hands. "Maguire, there's no reason to be a crap monster. I messed up. I get that."

He cocks his head to the side, his one brow raised higher than the other. "Do you, darlin'? Because those guys were ready to pounce on you. I was asked one thing—to protect you. The last thing my son asked of me. I could have lost you last night. Those men, they were ready to tear you apart."

I try to stand, but the stomach acid once more dictates my way to the bathroom. I have nothing to throw up. Only bile.

A knock on the bathroom door only pisses me off. "If you're going to lecture me anymore, you can shove it where the sun doesn't shine."

I can hear him clear his throat behind the door. "No, darlin', I'm done—just making sure you're okay."

I don't answer because right now it's easier to be mad at the jackass than the man who calls me darlin'.

CHAPTER 8

Maguire

Was I a prick? Fuck yeah, I was. My mind is still stuck on the men who were undressing Holland with their eyes—it's ingrained in my mind. And I don't like it, not one little bit. But of course, like the sick fucker I am, I still have images of her in those shorts, her ass hanging out.

She rarely dresses to show off the body she has. But last night, I saw more than I ever needed to, yet, *I craved more*. I wanted more. My son should come back to this earth just to kick my ass.

And when she cried, my heart broke for her. What is this girl, only twenty-one and yet she's dealing with the shit life has slung at her? I had watched her, for a good hour, her breathing regulated after she expelled everything in her stomach. And still, in that form, I couldn't take my eyes from her.

I learned so much about this girl. She mumbles in her sleep and moans. And of course, her sweet yet elicit moans had my cock growing by the minute, getting harder than steel. Her nose twitches in her sleep like she's Sabrina the teenage witch. And the most erotic thing, her fingers play with her nipples as they pebble. I tried to look away and I sure as fuck should have. I wanted to unzip my pants—jacking off to such a sight but I couldn't. I was stilled by it all. It's not all physical. The emotional connection of protecting her from those fucktards at the bar has only further strengthened our bond.

Sleep finally overtook me, but I didn't leave the girl alone. No, she's my responsibility and yet she's become more than a simple promise to my late son. I'm one sick shithead and I'm not sure how to ward off the beast that's overtaking me.

After I try to backpedal from my prick-like ways, she pretty much dismisses me when she pukes more. I didn't think her tiny little body could keep so much poison in her system, but it has.

I'm out in Scott's truck, waiting for her when I pull down the visor to block the wicked sun. A picture falls into my lap—it's Holland and Scott. She's looking at him, not at the camera. Her eyes, though they aren't straight on, tell me everything I've ever needed to know concerning my son and his wife. His eyes are locked on the camera, yet his arms are wrapped around her.

Rubbing the back of my neck, my own guilt for ogling my daughter-in-law hits me, even more, when she swings the door open, her eyes puffy. An apple aroma fills the cab of the truck. When she settles in, she keeps her eyes on the passenger door, even when she buckles her seat belt.

"Are you feeling better?"

She snickers. What could she snicker about right now? "Um, it depends, are you done being a jackass?"

She's still not looking in my direction and I chuckle

at her question. "I'm not sure how one thing affects the other. Me being a dick or not has nothing to do with if you *are* or *are not* feeling better."

"Crap on a stick," she says under her breath. "You are as much of an ass as your son could be at times."

Being compared to Scott leaves my heart broken, yet again. Will I ever wake with the thoughts of my son being gone and not feel like I'm a complete mess? Though, I can't help but smile at her comparison.

"And yes, Holland, to answer your question, I'm done being a prick." I stare at her, willing her to look at me. The picture of Scott and her is still in my lap.

"Well, I guess you're right, the two don't really correspond. I still feel like hot poop on a stick and I can't guarantee I won't puke again."

I place the picture back where it came from. I'm not sure if this is a needed reminder of what Holland has lost or the needed *reminder* of what they shared. Or the fucking *reminder* that she's my son's wife.

"I'll pull over the second you need me to, okay?"

"Thanks, Sarge." It's all she says and the little episode is behind us. I wish I could put everything she does to my body behind me. If it were only that easy.

It had taken ten minutes for Holland to fall asleep. Her purple ends are covering her face when an out and out snore fills the cab of the truck. Hell, this girl is so funny. She's cute, but she has these real-life qualities that should make her less appealing. For me, it only makes her more attractive. The girl is loud as fuck and her snore validates this little idiosyncrasy in her.

I'm in my own mind, Jon Bon Jovi and me singing "Living on a Prayer," when out of the corner of my eye, she pops out of a deep sleep. "Maguire, pull over, now." Her cries put me on notice and when I look in the rearview mirror with no one behind me, I pull over on the shoulder a bit more aggressively than I would typically.

The door on her side flies open and she leans her small body over, the sounds of puking can be heard for miles. When it's safe to get to her side of the truck, I pull her out, bringing her in close to me. This is more than a hangover.

"Holland, this is important," I whisper into her ear, cries flowing from her. "Did you take drinks from those fuckers or leave your drink somewhere?" It's a question that could be answered now that we are miles from those shitheads.

She leans back. "No, Scott taught me well. He pounded it in my head." Good boy, I think in the second when my son's wife's apple shampoo wafts into my nose.

"And you swear you only had a couple drinks?"

Her eyes are now big. "Yeah, and there was more Coke than rum, it was really watered down," she insists. "I swear, Maguire, I was just trying to forget all of this, that's all."

I push her hair from her face. "Okay, darlin', new plan. We're going to get another hour or two up the road, then we'll stop. I can add another day to the trip. All of this stress has caught up with you."

I release her and am about to walk around the rear of the truck. I stop when a big rig passes us. I turn to wait to hear her and sees she has more tears in her eyes. "That's another couple hundred dollars for a hotel room and food. I can't ask you…"

She's biting her nails and looking down at the ground. Her anxiety washes over her and I wonder if she's internally calculating everything she thinks she owes me. The idea of Holland's incessant worry triggers the protector in me to rush back to her, taking her in my arms. But I stay— my feet planted. "Holland, I'm not worried about a couple hundred bucks. Your health is more important." I don't give her more time to argue with me. And when she settles herself into the truck again, I'm hit with the fight we'd had earlier. She has been telling me the truth, all along. Suddenly, I'm a fucker for making this bereaved widow feel like a little kid.

"Darlin', I'm sorry I was such a fucking prick earlier."

A little chuckle escapes her mouth. I'm unable to look over at her, merging back onto the freeway. "Yeah, you were a fucking prick," she agrees.

This time, I let out a chuckle. "I still don't like you saying the word, fuck," I insist.

"Yeah, yeah, I'll take that under advisement, Sarge." I'm not sure why she calls me Sarge. It started when she was pissed at me. But somewhere deep down, I love she has a nickname just for me.

He's pulling into his signature Bates' Motel for the night and I cringe. I'm not out for his money, but Scott shared with me once how much Maguire is worth. He may not be a multi-millionaire, but he makes pretty good money. When he tried to talk Scott into joining him, he shared he could be a one-third owner with a doable pay in. It would take ten years, but he'd be looking at making three hundred thousand a year just in dividends—not counting his yearly salary.

It boggles my mind to stay in such a place, but it's this little thing in him that helps me feel a bit closer to Scott. It's wrong, placing all this on Maguire to be that part of Scott I miss so fucking much.

I don't care if he doesn't like me saying that word. I laugh, knowing how I can get under his skin a bit. And hell, there it is, all these emotions about Scott and Maguire emerging.

He doesn't know I'm awake, not a bit when he quietly opens the door to go pay. I sit, waiting for him, as I think of this adventure I'm on. It's different and I hate myself because I'm excited—working in design along with going to school to hone my craft. I take in a deep and pained cleansing breath. The guilt is eating at me. It has to be the reason I'm so sick. As Maguire had said, the stress has gotten to me.

He emerges from Norman Bates' office and I hurry to him, grabbing my key, running up the outdoor stairs, barely getting the key in to open the door. As I dash to the toilet to dispel my guts again, the only thing I can think is, *do they still make keys for motels?* This place is older than dirt.

A knock on the door is the only reason I pull myself off of the floor.

"Darlin'?"

Of course, it's Maguire, who else would it be? Grabbing for a towel, I don't have time to look at it to judge its cleanliness, I wipe the puke from my lips and fall onto the bed.

"Shit, Holland, you're still puking? I'd think you'd have nothing else in your system." He kneels next to me. His touch is on my head, checking me for a fever like Scott had done if I got sick, which was seldom. It's still a tender memory I cling to. And this is so eerily similar to my husband's touch. "I'm heading to the store; you must be dehydrated. Let's get you some saltines and Gatorade."

"Wait, don't forget my sewing machine." He had brought it up to his room last night.

"Don't worry, darlin', I got you." Somehow, I believe him.

CHAPTER 9

Maguire

After she drinks a quarter of the Gatorade and takes a Dramamine, she's asleep. I've been hovering over her like a mother hen. But I can't ignore the hunger pains in my own stomach.

I leave a little note—explaining I'm heading to the diner up the road. I have this sixth sense to sniff out the best little diners to get supper whenever I happen to be on a trip. Walking into what most would think is a hole in the wall, I can smell the grease that makes this place what most miss.

Ordering a bland turkey on wheat for Holland and the juiciest bacon cheeseburger for myself, my text alert gets my attention. Grabbing it quickly to check for a possible message from Holland, I see it's from Kat.

Kat was ready to drop everything to be here for me when I called her from the airport. But, neither one of us signed on for this. Sure, if everything had been local, it would have been different.

I try to find that little smile that normally comes out just for Kat. Under normal circumstances, the smile had always appeared because I knew I'd be getting some. She's great in bed. I do care for her, but her ex messed her up as much as Christine had with me. I open up the text and read it, wondering if what we have will change now with Holland in my life.

Kat: Hey, babe. I've been thinking about you a lot. I know this isn't what we do, but if you need to talk, I'm here for you.

I don't know what to do with her words. She still has parent status and *mine's gone*. It's not her fault, nor can I go through life ridding myself of friends based solely on the fact they still have their kids and I don't. I reply the only way I know how.

Me: Thanks. I'm dealing, little by little.

The bubbles appear under my last text.

Kat: I figured. Shit, Maguire, I have no idea what you're going through. I wish I could take this pain away.

Oh, if it were that simple.

Me: I know, I appreciate it, I do.

The bottom line, she doesn't understand. Soon the next text comes through.

Kat: I saw Ned at the grocery store. I'm glad he was there for you. But he said you're bringing Scott's truck home. I hate you're driving cross-country by yourself. I would have come out to help you.

Well, shit. I wonder if Kat will get all territorial? This is an issue I can tackle when we get home. She and I aren't exclusive, though she's been my steady friend with benefits for a while now. I send her a simple, non-descript message.

Me: Driving it cross-country—it's a great way to heal. I'll let you know when I'm back in town.

I pocket the phone, grabbing our dinner, putting the truck in drive, and getting back to the Bates' Motel as

Holland kept on calling it through her puking fits. I don't think she realized she had been complaining.

There are ambulances and a couple of squad cars when I pull into the motel parking lot. I'm out of the vehicle the second I place the truck into park. One ambulance has shut the back doors as I rush to it. "Sir, are you Maguire Parrish?"

My heart falls, how'd they know my name unless... I nod my head up and down. "Your daughter called the ambulance—pain in her stomach caused her to double over. I think it scared her when she couldn't find you."

I don't correct him. "If you'd like, sir, you can follow the ambulance, I don't need a statement from you."

I run to my truck, still able to see the flashing lights. I'm sweating and it's not from the summer of the hot, humid fucking south I'm trapped in. My mind is on my son and his last words, *you're the only one I can trust.* Yep, I'm not making him proud. First, the sensations of Holland near me is so impossible to resist. Then I leave her to what, wake up with some horrible illness.

It's a small county hospital and I don't have far to go to park. Running in, I'm stopped by the nurse as the door to the ER closes. "I'm her only family," I say.

"I know, sir. Let the doctor look at her first. She's an adult and I can't let you back right away."

I sit down, wanting to kick something—anything — but getting booted from the ER is not what I need right now.

An hour—sixty minutes, I'm going out of my ever-loving mind. No matter how many times I ask Nurse Ratchet, she basically tells me to sit my ass down. I'm about to bug the cranky nurse again when my name is finally called. I almost run to the doctor.

"Mr. Parrish?"

I shake his hand, waiting for the details. "Is Holland okay?"

"Oh, yeah, she's fine. Severely dehydrated and in her condition, I'd suggest you make sure she's getting enough fluid. It's not uncommon to feel queasy. But for the baby's sake, we need to make sure she's drinking water often. Even if she's losing weight, it's okay. The baby will take what she or he needs from the mama."

I cock my head to the side. "Um, what are you saying?"

He looks at his clipboard and then back at me. "Well, shit. I got Holland and another patient mixed up for a second. My other patient's parents know—whereas you apparently don't." He turns a ghostly white.

"Are you telling me she's pregnant?"

He turns away. "Well, hell, officially, I can't tell you anything. And please, this could land me in quite the pickle along with the hospital…it's been a hell of a night."

"Can you unofficially let me know if the baby is okay?" He nods his head yes. I can't breathe. Yet, I'm about to jump up and down with excitement. My heartbeat is racing and I'm sweating. I lost Scott—nothing can ever replace my son, but he has left me a part of himself *before he left this world.*

"Mr. Parrish?"

I look up at the doctor—the poor tired man thinking we'll sue him. "Yeah, Doc, no problem. I won't say anything. I'll wait until Holland tells me. But at least I understand now." I continue, "Can I see her?"

"Sure, but we'll have to keep her overnight. I

understand y'all are driving cross-country. Try not to push her if you have the ability."

My smile doesn't fade from my face. A grandpa, I'm going to be a grandpa. "No problem, whatever Holland needs, Doc, she'll get it from me."

When I enter the room, Holland is asleep. I take a look at the overstuffed chair in the corner, trying it out since this will be my bed for the night. Holland is filling the entire room with her loud snores and I've never been so happy to hear them.

CHAPTER 10

I wake with my eyes adjusting to the sunshine filling the room. It all comes back to me, second by second. The ambulance ride, the pain, and the diagnosis. Hell, it hadn't been a blip on my radar. How did I not know? I'm turning into quite the parent already, never noticing my missed period.

I attempt to sit up in bed. Whatever the doctor gave me last night to stop the vomiting did me in. I've not slept so deeply since before finding out about Scott. Looking down, I notice my stomach, something I can't for the life of me get out of my mind. And why would I?

I'd been so mad at Scott for leaving me and yet he left me with something to forever remember him by. Something we made in love, one of the last things we'd done.

When he was home, only weeks before he died, we'd talked about starting a family. He wanted me to get through school first. And where I agreed with him, I wanted babies early, too—because a combination of Scott and me together made something incredible. It shouldn't surprise me that I'm pregnant. We barely left our bed. And through it all, I forgot my birth control on a couple of occasions.

Something in the room gets my attention and I turn to see the sleeping form of Maguire, for the second night in a row, snoozing in a chair. I'm watching him intently—how in the world does his neck turn that much to one side? Hell, he looks so uncomfortable.

Do I wake him or let him sleep where he'll cause irreversible damage to his body? I don't think about it long when I try to lower my voice—though many have told me in the past, I can't whisper to save my life.. He pops up from his chair, trying to adjust to the light and the fact he has forgotten where he is.

"Shhhh, Maguire, it's okay. We're in the hospital."

He's on his feet, at my bed, looking me over. "Oh, yeah, it took me a second to get my bearings, darlin'. They wouldn't tell me anything—what's going on with you?"

Oh, good, he doesn't know. I can wait to share all this with him. I need time to come to grips with this first. Is he going to be like me viewing this as my one solace to get me through my grief? Will he be pissed because he'll be saddled with another responsibility for what Scott asked of him?

"I feel like an ass wipe for worrying you." His eyes widen, his brows furrowed. "What, I didn't say the f word, at least."

He displays a wide grin as Scott had when I had amused him. "But no curse words seem right coming from your sweet lips." I'm waiting for him to understand his words and tone are delivered with a little more flirtation than is acceptable. But, fiddlesticks, what do the deities above know about my situation? It's messed up in one giant ball of gasses that make up this earth. I'm pregnant with my dead husband's baby and my father-in-law, the grandpa—makes my heart pitter-patter.

I skip over the little remark and smile because what can I do? Call him on it? It's probably the hormones that are making me oversensitive. But I'm not overly sensitive. I miss the one-on-one attention. I continue to smile, wondering how or what I should say.

"What did the doctors tell you?" he asks, rubbing my forearm.

"They are guessing it's stress." Sure, I'm omitting the obvious, but the truth is the ER doc did say under normal situations I probably wouldn't have let my body get so dehydrated. Plus, I certainly would have noticed a missing period. I'm always one for timeliness and my cycle takes after me on this attribute.

"Um, well, good to know." He stands, leaning over to give me a peck on the forehead. I still at first, isn't this odd? He's my father-in-law. He did this to me the first time I met him five years ago, though I'd only seen him a couple times since then. But why does my own breath hitch when his lips touch my skin? Can he sense the goosebumps as my skin pebbles? Can he see the sweat starting to form at the top of my head? Does he sense I stop breathing?

"Listen, darlin', I'm running to the hotel to pack up. We're slowing down our trip."

My hand, without thinking, is in front of him, attempting to stop him.

"No, darlin', you listen here. I have part of me that wants to take you to the nearest airport and fly you to Redding and have Ned, who you met at the funeral, pick you up and house you with his wife, Elise, and him. But you are

too fucking stubborn, and I don't have it in me to fight you."
He stops when my mouth is on the edge of forming some
witty comment. "And quite honestly, apparently I can't let
you out of my sight."

"Fuck, Maguire, I'm not some kid you can order
around. I don't need to be watched like I'm helpless."

"Holland," he deadpans.

"Maguire," I return, my tone matching his.

"You know how I feel about you swearing."

I scrunch my brows together. Is this man for real?

"Yeah, yeah, but the last time I checked, you're not
my daddy and I can take care of myself."

He walks to the door and turns around. "And how is
that working out for you—since you landed yourself in the
ER?" I think he's gone when he pops his head back in. "I'm
packing up at the hotel and my main goal is to get out of
fucking Georgia today since I feel like we're never leaving
the south." He leaves and I look up like I'm talking to Scott.

"Shit, Scott, you never told me your dad was as
moody as a girl on her period." I wait for a reply, but I get
none. That won't stop me from still talking to my husband.

Maguire

My dickishness came out full force. Am I really upset that
she's not been taking care of the baby, the one she had no
idea existed? And the last comment, *how is that working for
you*? What an ass thing to say.

The grandpa in me wants to drive back to Atlanta and
put her on a plane. I'd be doing it with her kicking and
screaming. Yeah, that's what is best for the baby. The baby

I already love with every fucking breath I breathe. But then I'd miss that mouthy and unreasonable woman.

And it can't be what's best for the baby when the mother is so pissed off, she'd turn into some sort of villain who'd be mad at me for the next several months.

As I pull myself out in Scott's truck, my heart is in competition for the peace that Holland gives it, the brokenness of losing my child and the healing it feels at the idea of Scott's child in this world.

I'm back at the hospital, she's sitting there with tears falling down her face. "Okay, Sarge, I'm here, waiting for your arrogant ass."

In my arm is a small suitcase, I'd grabbed her a change of clothes and toiletries. "Listen, darlin',"

I begin, and she stands quickly, grabbing her clothes and disappearing into the bathroom.

But, it's not before she says, "Save it, jackass."

This girl is so full of spunk, I let it go and sit down, rehashing our trip since we're only driving six hours a day. With my head in my phone and the atlas I'd brought in, I hear, "Hell, that stupid atlas, you know what I'd like to do with it?"

"Um, no, what would you like to do with it?" I stand, walking toward her, jokingly challenging her.

"Yeah, Maguire, you can shove it up your..."

She doesn't have a chance to finish her sentence when the doctor from last night walks in. "Miss Parrish?"

Though I'm indeed trying to joke with her, she's not returning the sentiment but turns to the doctor. "Yes, but *I'm Mrs. Parrish*, by the way," she begins.

"Um, I thought he was your father," he clarifies, looking between us.

"Father-in-law," she adds, and his look can't be avoided. I did lead everyone to think she was my daughter to get more information. "My husband just died, and this man somehow thinks he's my keeper." Oh, she's still pissed from earlier.

"Um." He leans into where he thinks only Holland can hear him. "Mrs. Parrish, do you feel safe with him?"

I laugh. This is the most ridiculous question ever and Holland giggles at him. "Actually, I do, Doctor. Thanks for your concern. The fact that he's an asshole from time to time doesn't mean that I don't feel safe in his presence plus he'd never hurt me."

Her words hit me, but I can't help but stop at her language.

"And yes, Maguire, I cursed, get the hell over it." This only makes her laugh and our little fight from earlier is over. The doctor asks for privacy. I'll keep up the illusion that I don't know about my grandchild she's carrying. I'll wait for her to tell me.

CHAPTER 11

H e's acting weird, getting the door for me. Saying we're slowing the trip down. We're still in Georgia, mere miles from Alabama. We're three days into this journey of ours and we should be somewhere in Arkansas. And this trip will last for years if we're not able to get some miles between North Carolina and us.

Two hours into the trip, we're on the outskirts of Birmingham, pulling into a Waffle House. This man and his need to eat at diners for every meal makes me crazy. "Tell me, do you eat like this normally?"

He twists his lips into a small smirk. "Oh, fuck no! I'd be the size of a house if I did. And for the next month, I'll be pulling double duty with my workouts." It makes me happy thinking of him *working out*.

The second my waffles are placed in front of me, I jet from the booth as quickly as I can, barely making it to the bathroom to vomit, like I have food in my system. This'll be a long nine months at this rate.

I'm gone for ten minutes and when I look at the booth, I can't find Maguire. He's at the doors, his cell phone in his hand, texting someone. He juts his chin toward the exit.

"Did you eat?" I ask.

"Quickly, I didn't figure you wanted to sit down with food again, so I tossed it back."

With my purple unicorn purse Scott bought for me off of some vendor in Bahrain, I toss a couple Lemonheads in my mouth. He holds the door for me as I adjust, passing me the seat belt to make sure I'm secure.

Waiting for him to get around to the front of the truck, he turns to me. "Darlin', you sure you're okay?"

"Yeah, whatever this is, it just needs to work itself out." I think of the little baby who's taking over my body. A smile takes over my face. With my arms hugging my stomach, I catch Maguire watching me with a broad grin.

He puts the truck into gear. "We're driving a little farther up the road and calling it a night. I need you to get some good rest." We're barely on the highway when it hits me. The doctor thought Maguire was my father.

It's quiet as the pieces are all fitting together. "Fuck, Maguire."

I don't get any other words out of my mouth before he turns. "Darlin', we've been through this—seriously, you're too pretty for those words." I'm quiet. "Why do you continue to utter the one word I hate to hear you say?"

"You're an ass. You know, don't you? The reason you're driving less today. Why you're insisting I get my rest? Smiling at me, all-knowing. You know I'm pregnant."

He downshifts and takes the next exit onto a lonely road, pulling over to the shoulder. With the truck in park, he turns his body toward me. "Listen, darlin'," he begins.

I don't wait to listen, I'm out the door, walking in some field. Not sure where I'm going. I'm not upset with him. But right now the perfect storm of emotions is about to collide.

Running after me, it's not hard for a man *Maguire's size* to catch up with a person *my size*, especially as sick as I've been.

"Holland, I wanted you to tell me when *you* were ready." He pulls at me and I stop. My body is facing away from him. "Please don't be upset with me."

"I'm not," I reply and the tears don't stop.

I turn when it all comes out at one time. Maguire pulls me into his embrace, and I allow it. "Then, darlin', what's all of this about? Aren't you happy?"

I wipe at my tears to avoid them staining his simple gray t-shirt. "No, it's not that... I'm happy. I'll have a part of Scott with me still." Why am I telling him, he must feel the same way? "But it doesn't make me miss him any less. Maybe more, because he'll miss out on everything." The storm, this convergence keeps coming. "And honestly, the idea of doing it alone scares the hell out of me."

He pulls back. "See, that's where you're wrong. So fucking wrong. You won't be going through it alone, I promise."

"But you have your whole life. You don't need to be saddled by your crazy daughter-in-law. *And her baby.*"

Moving a piece of my hair from my eyes, he pulls it back behind my ear. "See, again, you're wrong. I couldn't be there for Scott, but I sure as fuck will be there for my grandbaby." He tips my head farther so our eyes meet, and he continues, "And the mama of my grandbaby will always be someone who'll be a part of my life." His face is so close to mine, *his lips* are even closer to *my lips*. For a split second,

I think they will touch my own until a big rig drives by and honks at us. And for this split second, I feel like Jezebel in the Bible—a temptress—about to undo all of this in front of me. I break from his embrace, waiting for him in the cab of the truck as he, too, takes a couple minutes for himself.

He opens the door, starts the truck, and drives the next thirty minutes until we reach our destination for the night, neither one of us addressing what could have been— a new beginning or our undoing—on the side of the road.

Maguire

I'm left to some field in Alabama, speaking to my own demons. Four weeks is what it's been since I watched my son's casket lower into the ground. From there, it took almost that long to pack up Holland, taking care of all the small details. It's been a long month of us being thrust together. And in this time, did we really get *this close*? More so, was I close to kissing my son's wife? The woman who's carrying my one link to my Scott? She had walked away after the trucker beeped at us—like he knew the whole sordid soap opera which is now my life.

I take some deep breaths, watching the trees sway in front of me. They were almost witness to the worst mistake I could make. And yet, I still want it, I still want her.

Retreating to the truck, I look upon Holland, her face scrunched against the passenger window, looking anywhere but at me. Hoisting myself back into the cab, I stay silent, starting it, the hum of the engine is the only thing filling the quietness among us.

My mind is on the regret and remorse of me wanting

this girl. And that's what she is—a girl. It seems like five minutes to the reality of thirty when we pull up to the Embassy Suites for the night. I thought I'd treat her to something other than the Bates' Motel as she calls it. The gesture makes her smile, but we still have not spoken.

I leave her be, walking inside, securing two rooms—on two different floors—on entirely different sides of one another. When I run outside to give her the keycard, she merely says, "I'm exhausted. Don't count on me for dinner, I'll probably throw it up anyway. I still have crackers and Gatorade." She looks at her room number and disappears for the night.

Leaning against the bed of the truck, I internally moan, watching her disappear behind the door.

CHAPTER 12

Maguire

The letter, his last words are in my hands. Nowhere in it does it ask for me to fall for Holland, to kiss her in a field in Alabama. My life has been focused on my career. I'd done the wife and kid thing. Marriage certainly hadn't worked out. I can't regret it, though. I would not have had Scottie. And the memories, they assault me from day to day. Some days they are the only thing that gets me by. But, other days, they are salt in an angry wound, unwilling to heal.

On the edge of some cheap bed, I'm left to wonder about the father Scott could have been. Would he have sacrificed for him or her, like I was unwilling to do? Now that I have my business and a very successful one at that, was it worth it? Staying in Cali to continue, or following Christine like I should have?

But do I only regret this because Scott's no longer here and hindsight is 20/20? My eyes roam the letter, his pleas so vivid I can hear his voice. At the age of fourteen, we'd started work on his truck. He loved the piece of rusty metal more than anything and only he had a vision for it, one I didn't have. And I knew then, he loved that piece of junk we worked years to restore. Then, when he called me to tell me about this girl—or in his words—*the* girl, I asked how he knew it was real. His reply is still ingrained in my memory. *"Dad, I love her more than my truck."* I knew it was true love then, to love Holland more than his most prized possession in this world. I see how it's possible with Holland—she's so easy to love. Even in her more animated features, which could drive most people insane, I only find them endearing. My eyes don't leave the letter, the one I try to burn into memory, as I attempt to honor my son's last wish. I leave her be for the night—taking her at her word that she needs to sleep.

The text alert goes off on the nightstand of my hotel room. A towel is around my waist when I leave the bathroom and make my way to the jeans and t-shirt I have waiting for me on the bed. It's my standard attire. On the rare occasion Kat and I go out, I may put on a button-down top. But combat boots, it's all this carpenter knows. Waiting to check my phone until I'm fully dressed, the beeps continue. I stop what I'm doing, in case it's Holland—something with the baby.

In the ten seconds it takes to cross the room to my phone, my mind is in overdrive about how cruel fate would be to give us this glimmer of hope only to have it taken away in a miscarriage. I say a silent prayer to the man upstairs. I know I for one couldn't take it. Holland, she'd crumble. Hell, there's no one tougher than her—but a person, even one as strong as my daughter-in-law, can only take so much. Maybe if I call her this more often, these odd feelings I have toward her might dissipate.

By the time I get to my phone, the worst-case scenarios are rumbling through my mind. Picking it up, I read the first text.

Darlin': Come on, Old Man, at this rate we may make it to California by Christmas.

I scroll down, the next text is just as snarky.

Darlin': Oh, no, you either died of old age or you can't get to your cane.

I'm wondering in her smart-ass-ness if she's feeling any better.

Me: Yeah, yeah, don't be a brat. Keep it up and I'll leave you on the side of the road.

Darlin': Well, you wanted to get an early start. It's seven a. m. Let's get going or I'm heading back to bed.

Me: Listen, brat, I'm getting dressed. See you in five.

I toss my phone down, wondering if Holland is having images of me dressing. It had not been my intention—not in the least, but now *I'm thinking of her* half-dressed.

I stare at his last text. He's getting dressed. What's wrong with me? I'm in mourning. My stomach is upset and my chest tight. This has nothing to do with morning sickness. I miss Scott so much. Last night, I cried myself to sleep for the baby of ours he'll never hold. The guilt had continued when I could still feel Maguire's breath on my skin.

I'm in the truck, waiting for him and what's more, I want to see him. I miss how his eyes, the hazel green of them, penetrate through me.

I don't have much time to think when the door opens, and he slings himself into the truck. The man must own a V-neck in every color. And his combat boots, it's all he wears. I guess it makes sense, building stuff all day long.

"Morning, Holland." My heart falls a little. I miss the term darlin', it's the panty melting tone along with the one word that puts me on notice this man is more to me than a father-in-law.

"Good morning, Sarge." My own tone is a little more clipped than I mean for it to be. Holy hell, what in the world? Am I really upset he didn't call me darlin'?

His hand changes the radio station. This old beat up pickup truck has serious radio along with kick-ass bass. Scott insisted on the best. He changes what I have been listening to, he must have the same rule Scott had. Whoever is driving, picks the music. In the maybe twelve hours we've been on the road, I've been too out of it to really care. It starts just enough to hear one of my favorite bands, The Front Bottoms with "Flashlight."

"Hey," I whine.

"I drive, I decide." He's not smiling, he's dead serious. Yes, I'm right. Yet, another freaking similarity. All of a sudden, some sort of bad metal hits me, and I shake my head—the same flipping music.

"Anyway, darlin', I don't listen to EMU music."

As he's turning out of our hotel—I'm breaking into hysterics.

"What. What's so fucking funny?" But he's laughing at me as I'm laughing at him.

"Um, Emu, that's a bird. It's EMO."

He shrugs at me. "Yeah, what can I say, I'm old. I'm not up to date on all that shit and stuff. I just know what I like." He starts singing along with "Enter Sandman." It makes me smile.

"So what's got you grinning over there? Is it Metallica?" he asks.

I push a piece of hair from my eyes, listening to the same lyrics Scott would sing while tinkering on this truck. "Um, did you know this was Scott's go-to music?"

His head turns quickly to me, then back at the road. "No shit, really?"

"Yeah. This was Scott's truck work song. Sometimes he'd put it on repeat and after ten times, Mark would wander out of his house, giving Scott hell. Telling him he was a millennial and to start acting like one. Scott would tell him to eff off and they'd sit with a beer, listening to the song on repeat just so Scott could goad Mark and every other person on our cul-de-sac."

I don't know I'm crying until drops land on my arms as fast as raindrops. "Fuck, I miss him so much." It comes out so naturally and I wait for Maguire to challenge me.

"I'll let that one slide, darlin'," he replies. When I twist my head to him, he, too, has uncontrolled tears. I remain quiet as both of us reminisce together in our silence.

When my tears stop after thirty minutes, I don't realize I'm singing along to "Blaze of Glory," when Maguire starts to sing with me.

"Are you feeling better today?" he asks in the middle of the chorus.

"Yeah, a little." Rummaging through my purse, I grab a pack of Lemonheads, popping a couple into my mouth. "I can stomach these and saltines and ginger ale."

He glances at the sugary treat and shakes his head.

"My grandchild needs more nutrients than those three things."

I toss a couple more Lemonheads in my mouth. "What? I'm getting all my vitamin C," I tease. "No, seriously, the doctor told me to make sure I drink and eat when I can. Believe me, this baby is my first priority."

His eyes stay on the road while he finishes up the song. He turns off the radio, clearing his throat. "Um, Holland, mind me asking you a little bit of a personal question?"

This causes me to almost choke on my candy. "Well," I begin, still coughing a bit. "Sure, I guess, but I reserve the right to plead the fifth, just in case," I say, trying to offset my nervousness.

"Fair enough." I watch his profile and his Adam's apple as he swallows. "Scott—was he a good husband to you? I wasn't able to show him *how to be a good husband.* And it's one of the many things I regret."

I don't think when my hand reaches for his arm. "Maguire, Scott was the best husband I could have ever asked for. He saw you—the good man you are and followed in your footsteps. You may not have been a husband, but you were the man he needed. Believe me, you did very well."

Maguire pulls over on the side of the freeway. I remove my arm as his face drops to the steering wheel. Throughout the funeral, I barely saw more than a tear from his eyes. Though there were times he would excuse himself. I'd hoped in his time of solitude, he was using it as an outlet, getting it out.

Unbuckling my seat belt, I scoot over to him, grateful for the bench seat of this truck. I rub his back in a circular motion as he lets it all out. I can't help but feel honored, he's allowing me to see him in this state. Yet, it's heartbreaking—

this strong man coming undone at the seams.

I sit here, my hand on his back, being a comfort for him because he's been that for me more times than I can count.

CHAPTER 13

After Maguire's breakdown, we drive for two hours in silence until we stop for gas. Maguire insists this truck gets pretty good gas mileage, but I think he's full of shit, with how often we are breaking for fuel.

He never shied away from me, though he'd been quiet, but in the solitude of the cab, I only think of what my baby will look like. Will he have the same eyes as his or her daddy's? Will she be tall like Scott or short like me? More importantly, will our child have the tender heart of his or her father. Looking over at the grandpa of my child, Scott had the same loving nature of his own father. I hope the odds are in my favor.

When we refuel, he brings me more Lemonheads. We barely get started up the road when he asks, "Tell me to mind my own business if I cross the line, but had you two always wanted children? I mean, I missed so much of Scott. I'm trying to figure him out as a man."

I get it, after his breakdown, I think it's more of what

he didn't get to see in him. "Unless you ask about our sex life, Maguire, I'll share anything you want to know." It comes out so casually. I don't blush like I think I should. I mean, obviously, Scott and I were together for five years and we had crazy fun sex.

"Yeah, you can rest assured, darlin', I won't touch that subject with a ten-foot pole." We both laugh and I turn to him, to answer his original question.

"We wanted at least three. With both of us being only children, we wanted more for our kids." I look at my stomach. This will probably be my only child and it makes me hurt for him or her. "But yeah, it was something I wanted sooner than him. He wanted to get through the Army, move to California, and put me through school. He told me five years. And I was okay waiting, but—it's been a little more than a day and my life has changed overnight. And now, it's all I can think about."

When he doesn't say anything, I look over to him and he's smiling. "What about you, Gramps?"

His concentration is on the road, but he begins, "Nothing can ever replace Scott, but shit, there will be a part of my son running around for me to see. I meant it, Holland, I didn't get to be a dad—not the kind I wanted. But I'll be that grandpa. You better get used to an overbearing father-in-law, because this baby will get everything it needs from me."

This makes me happy. My baby certainly won't get any attention from my parents. Then I think of the crazy overbearing grandma Christine will be. I can't, not in this minute, consider her. And I reply to Maguire, "I'll take all the help I can get, but you'll have to run interference with Christine."

He outwardly groans.

"Hey, since you two were planning for children, does it mean you have names picked out?"

The grief hits in waves and I can't explain why this one little question hurts so much. I smile, I don't want to cry. I've made it a couple hours.

"Well, yeah, we did, but I'd like to keep this part to myself, just a little bit longer."

I've been around him enough; I understand sincerity when it's plastered on his face. Patting my hand, he smiles, "I get it. I understand. Just know—you need anything, I'll make it happen."

He says this as if I hung the moon. But for him, in his grief, this is the shooting star that may get us both through the worst time in our lives.

We're finally in Arkansas. It's only taken us five days and yet, we're still twenty-one hundred miles from Coral Creek, California. And because he only wants to drive six hours a day, we find ourselves in Clarksville, Arkansas, around three p.m. We've barely stopped, only to get a couple snacks along the way. Somehow, we're being upgraded from Norman Bates to first class, this time Maguire checks us in at a Hilton Suites for the night. It's still unholy hot outside and the first thing I notice is the swimming pool.

I walk to my room, with not so much as a goodbye to Maguire, not for any other reason than I'm comfortable enough around him. We don't need this formality; it further indicates the familiarity and ease of our relationship. Even when he's challenging me and he's a prick, there's still a calmness between us.

In my room, I find my bikini right away. Surmising

I need a little trim, I hop in the shower quickly. Looking down at my stomach, I wonder if this will be the last time I wear a bikini for a while. I don't care—I have a baby growing in my belly and for the first time in weeks, the tears falling like the water in the shower are those of happiness.

With the lion under control, I pull on my light lavender polka-dotted swimsuit and my short shorts. Leaving for the pool, a couple catcalls are directed my way. I ignore them. There's only one person I want to turn on and he's no longer here. But, is this true, I wonder, thinking of another person who turns me on quickly with one up and down of his eyes.

I dive into the water, making my way to the surface, I turn to my back, floating for once, not a care in the world for about ten seconds. It's the water and the bright sun making me forget everything. Splashes and movement in the pool alert me that people have jumped in, one too close to me and the baby I will protect with all I have.

Being on my back, I turn my entire body into the water. I stare over to the next person who's jumped way too close to me and I move my head from side to side. I'm surrounded by three huge men. I'd typically classify them as cute, but in the here and now, they're only pissing me off. I attempt to swim past one and his buddy and him block my path.

"Hey, honey," the one man says and I again notice he's a good-looking man. It doesn't negate the fact that they were too close to jumping on me.

"Hey yourself, asswipe," I return, trying a different direction when another buddy of his blocks my path. I move back to the center of the pool. "Listen, guys, I'm not your conquest today. As a matter of fact, you've just fucked with the wrong mama bear."

"Oh, she's feisty, this one," one of the men swimming near me says.

"Yeah, and this feisty one, as you call it," I pause, "is pregnant and you almost jumped on me." I swim past them this time, my words paralyzing them. "So I suggest you leave me the fuck alone or you are going to get one angry man down here in about two minutes. And believe me, you don't want to fuck with him. He's as protective of this baby as I am—if not more."

One of the men now has his eyes fixed on my wedding ring. He swims toward the stairs. "Sorry, little lady, we had no idea." He looks at his little posse, whistling toward them. "Come on, guys, I don't feel like dealing with an overprotective alpha male daddy today." All three men grab towels and exit the pool. I smile and return to floating on my back.

Maguire

I look out at the small little town and as I do, I have a view of the swimming pool. I'm about to admire my daughter-in-law in her skimpy swimsuit until my blood reaches an intensity of anger and rage. My pulse races and my heartbeat pounds. "What the fuck?" I'm out of the room, taking the stairs three at a time. I'm cracking my knuckles, barreling toward those three fuckers who have Holland surrounded in the pool. I'm limbering up my shoulders, about ready to take a fucker's head off. I bypass the lobby and thunder toward the pool area. When I storm through the double doors, I'm met with Holland floating on her back.

I sit in a chair, close to the pool, summoning every

calming molecule I can to emerge. If not, I'll go from room to room looking for those men who thought they'd get a little piece of my daughter-in-law. She turns over, unaware I'm near her, swimming under the water, coming up the side near me. As her eyes adjust to the light, a little smile appears on her face.

"Well, this is a bit creepy. Are you going to sit there or are you coming in?"

I chuckle. "Yeah, I guess you're right, I thought you needed me, but it's obvious you can take care of yourself. By the way, you saved those guys' lives—you know, right?" I ask.

"Yeah, I told them you'd be down here in a couple minutes, kicking ass if they continued. I guess I dabble in prophecy," Holland deadpans.

"Or you understand I would do anything in this world to keep my promise."

She nods with an all-knowing look. But there's more. She doesn't belong to anyone else and yet she doesn't belong to me either. So why do I want to call her mine? It's more. I want to do my best caveman impression, slinging her over my shoulder—never letting her go.

"Well, thanks for your concern, but as you already admitted, I can take care of myself."

Her reply is snarky, clipped, and I'm not sure what to do with it.

"Since my services are no longer needed, I'm going to read for a bit."

"Wait!" she cries after me. I twist my body around, hoping she's about to ask me to stay. "You read?" she asks.

I'm not sure if I should be amused or insulted. "*Yes, Holland*, I'm an avid reader." Now, with my own reply, I'm the one with a clipped tone. "Why does this surprise you?"

She shrugs her shoulders. "It doesn't. Scott always had a book with him. He actually bought big jackets so the books would fit in his coat pockets."

What the actual fuck? What more had I missed in my son's life? "Scott was a reader?" I had him for a month twice a year and where I'd see him with a few books, I didn't see him with many.

"Um, yeah. But it was something Scott started to embrace after high school. He was a poor student, but it wasn't for his lack of trying. When he joined the Army, he realized he had some learning disabilities—dyslexia being one of them. When he found ways to compensate for it, he started reading a lot more. He'd always loved it, but it was too hard."

I'm walking back to Holland, wanting and needing more. "I mean, I knew he struggled in school. Christine didn't think he applied himself, yet, I always knew he was smart."

"He was ashamed of his learning disabilities and shared it with no one but me."

I pull out the chair and almost throw myself into it. "I missed out on so much of my son's life. What books did he like? What did he like to read?"

She purses her lips. "I should know it by heart. He talked about this series all the time. I even tried to pick it up, but I'm not into sci-fi. It had something to do with Mars— Red something."

"*Red Rising* by Pierce Brown?" I ask, my voice elevated.

"That's it." She smiles. "What, you know that book?"

"Yeah, I'm re-reading the series. The fourth book came out earlier this year and I've read it, but needed a recap," I add, reeling from the fact that Scott loved to read—and the same books, too.

"Well, see it's nature vs. nurture at its finest," Holland adds, pushing herself off the wall, floating on her back again. And I'm left to think of all the conversations I lost out on. I'm sad, but he had so much of me in him and that gives me comfort.

CHAPTER 14

Maguire

We're in California. After driving for three days from Clarksville, we stayed in Amarillo then some small, and I mean, small-ass, town off the interstate in Arizona. At least now we're in the right state. From Bakersfield, where we stayed last night, it's a straight shot north until we make it to my place.

"Listen, darlin'," I begin when Holland meets me in the truck, a pair of cut-off shorts and this amazingly tight purple tank top, matching the ends of her hair. She never dresses this provocatively and it's eye-catching. "It's about eight hours from here. We can break it up or just push through," I suggest.

She smiles and I'm met with an evil, sinister look. I brace myself because I'm not sure what she'll say. "Look, I love this truck of Scott's so much, but if I spend one more fucking day in it, I'll lose it."

Cocking my head to the side, I begin, "Holland."

"Yeah, yeah, I get it. You don't like the F-word coming from my pretty lips." Now she's mocking me. "But you realize, Benedict Arnold, you're a hypocrite. You say it like it's as common as words like the or and. So...there's that. Plus, I'm twenty-one years old and if I want to swear like a fucking sailor, I fucking will." She gives me a small smile through her little outburst.

"First off, you're aware that Benedict Arnold was a traitor and not a hypocrite?" Her intense scowl lets me know I've messed with her on the wrong day, but I chuckle at her anyway.

She places her middle finger up in my face. "Well, I'm sure he was a fucking hypocrite, too, then."

"Semantics aside, you're too good for it." I pause like I have more to say. Holland waits and I finally continue, "Anyway, I take it you just want to drive right through." The motor is on and we are enjoying the air conditioning when my text alerts start chirping. I look down at the message, a mixture of emotions hitting me when I see who it is. "So?" I ask, ignoring the text when another one comes through.

"Yeah, let's just get this trip over with," she replies. She glances toward my phone, and another one comes through. "Who's texting you and why are you ignoring it?"

"Um, just a friend wanting to know when I'll be home," I admit.

Her stare stays on me. "This many texts, I'd say it's more than just a friend. I had no idea you had a girlfriend." Her tone changes when she says the word girlfriend.

I'm quick to stop this conversation but also to halt her assumptions. "I don't have a girlfriend, darlin'."

When she doesn't turn her head, but only her eyes, her reply is flat. "Okay, if you say so. But someone is pretty damn quick to be texting you first thing this morning."

After eight days in this truck, close proximity and all that shit, I've realized Holland doesn't do mornings.

However, she'll have to get up earlier than this when she starts work. "What are you gonna do when you begin work?" I ask. I hope she doesn't notice I'm attempting to change the subject.

"Nice one, Sarge. First off, when I begin work, I won't be stuck in this truck with you for days on end." The little kid in her surfaces when she sticks her tongue out. She takes in a deep breath, pushing her loose curls from her face when her voice turns a little sterner. "Don't think I don't know what you're doing. Seriously, who's texting you at seven in the morning?"

Fuck, we aren't even on the freeway and I'm attempting to stop this conversation. "It's just a friend of mine, seeing if I need anything. Offered to bring in some groceries. Turn down the AC. Things like that."

Her smile tightens, it doesn't reach her eyes. "I see. And let me guess—this friend is a female."

Well, hell, she'll meet Kat once I get around to setting something up. Truth is, I have no desire to share what I once had with Kat, not now. Maybe not ever. It hasn't ever been more than sex. I don't answer and she continues, "So, this apartment you have above the garage. What's it like?"

I haven't told her about the condition of the apartment above my garage. "About that, Ned went out there last week to see what needs to be done to make it livable. I mean, I wasn't planning on it being used for a couple more years." She stiffens with this news I'd not been ready to give her. "He has contractors called. He's set it all up, but it'll take weeks before you can move in. So, until then, I'm going to put you in Scott's old room."

She bends down, picking up her purse to pop a Lemonhead into her mouth. "Let me get this straight, I'll be living in your house until the apartment is fixed." She tosses another yellow candy into her mouth and I nod my head in agreement. "And through this time, your friend, who is a girl, will be popping in and out of the house, for the benefits y'all have agreed upon?"

Now it's my turn to stiffen. It's something my son may have disclosed to his wife. Scott understood I didn't do attachments. He'd often call my gals, not that I've had many, my friends with benefits. It's something that didn't bother me, my son knowing, after all, he was an adult when he put it together. But it irritates the fuck out of me for Holland to know.

"First off, darlin', no one is going to pop in the house unless it's Ned, my business partner and best friend. And he normally calls. And as for my *friend*, you don't have to worry about overnight visits." And why the hell am I explaining this to her, she's not in the need to know.

I put the truck in gear, peeling out of the parking lot. Fuck, the last eight hours will be the longest.

Why does it bother me so much? Maguire having a girlfriend or *fuck buddy* shouldn't get under the very core of my skin—but it does. And maybe it's the secrecy. Listen to me whine. What business is it of mine? *It's not my business*—one freaking bit. Yet, I'm making it mine.

My eyes are locked on the outside, anything but this truck and the incessant eighties rock that's overtaking my brain. As "Welcome to the Jungle" fills the cab, a vein pulses at the side of my neck when my anger reaches a boiling point. I lean forward and push the button to stop Axl Rose's voice.

"Certainly, darlin', interrupt Axl—it's not like I'm listening to him." His pitch is so condescending. Why should I worry he's porking some bimbo just to have sex? But I'm more pissed off than I should be.

"Oh, stop being a jerk for one second, I have something to say."

He motions to the middle of the seat. "Well, the floor is all yours, say your piece."

"Before you started acting like a jackass—it's your house. You want to bring your friend who's a girl into your home, it's no skin off my back."

A smile widens on his face.

"What did I say that's so funny?" I question.

He shakes his head before he replies, "Well, thanks for giving me permission to have a playdate whenever I deem fit at my *own* house."

I physically turn my body from him as he takes the next turn, pulling into a gas station. "Be a jerk, I don't care. I was feeling bad for throwing a hissy fit earlier." It's so easy being upset with him right now. And I'm actually glad he's a douche.

Slowing down the truck, I feel his finger gently poking my shoulder. "Darlin', my house is yours. I'll do anything to make you feel wanted, needed, and always a part of my family." He's out of the truck so fast. I'm no longer mad. His words are kind and I want to melt into them. Shitake mushrooms, it's easier when he's a monster prick and not the sweet man I grow closer to every day I'm with him.

I wake to "Summer of '69" when we hit a couple potholes. Taking in my surroundings, I notice we're on a back road. It's close to five p.m. "Where are we?" I must have been sleeping for three hours and my neck is tight. Moving my hands up to massage the sore muscles, he leans forward to turn the blaring voice of Bryan Adams off.

"Hey, darlin'." He's smiling, and the scruff on his face is intoxicating. "We're about a mile from my house."

I know nothing about his home. Scott still visited him after we were married, and he came by himself. He hated to be away from me, but I encouraged one-on-one time with his dad.

"We're in the boondocks?" I question, getting acquainted with my new surroundings.

"Yeah, I like my space. My house is small, don't need much but I have several acres. I'm not far from Shasta Lake." The truck climbs up a small incline nestled in the hills. I take in all the green around me. In the south, all the grass turns to brown by this time of the year.

Winding up a small little hill, I get the first glance of my father-in-law's estate. With as much land as my eyes can take in, it's not just a house. We pull straight ahead into a large gravel driveway. His grass around his property is freshly mowed and trimmed. On one side of the driveway is a large garage, at least three times as big as his house. To the right is his much smaller house. He wasn't joking about having a small home.

"Home sweet home, darlin'," he croons, pulling up to the front deck. "I have never been so glad to see my house." He's out of the truck, a large golden retriever almost galloping toward him. I'm still in the cab taking in the peace and beauty of this place. It's a retreat, a beautiful haven. No one will ever bug us here. It's out of the way. I'm about to let myself out of the cab when a beautiful tall blonde emerges from the front door. There's a smile on her face while she's hugging Maguire when her eyes settle on me.

The open deck leads to the front with floor-to-ceiling windows. A deep wood frames the outside and the porch is fully covered, protecting everyone from the California sun. And although it's a beautiful little bungalow, my eyes are fixed on the tall blonde pulling Maguire into her perfect little body.

I don't see his facial features since his fine ass is facing me, but his entire body stiffens. This unknown woman whispers in his ear and he turns around, waving at me to meet his sex buddy. Opening the door, I slowly peel myself off the seat and bring my purse with me.

"Holland, I'd like you to meet my friend, Kat." With the look on Kat's face, she has not been expecting me.

"Oh, M, I had no idea your daughter-in-law was visiting." Her voice is too perky, like her perky boobs. And I'm already calling bullshit on them being real. She's too thin to sport those huge tits that are falling out of her tight pink tank top.

I don't wait for "M" to reply. I hate that—stupid M, his name is Maguire and it's a cool as hell name, why shorten it? "I'm not visiting. I'm moving here. Taking the apartment above the garage." I extend my arm to shake her hand and she's looking at "M" for a reaction.

"Oh, this makes sense." Her voice is too sugary. "By the way, Holland, I'm so sorry for your loss. And thanks for the sacrifice you and your late husband made for our country. You both are the true heroes."

Well, hell, now she's acting nice as his dog comes to greet Maguire. He kneels down. "Hey, boy, missed me?" His voice changes from his tough guy vibrato to one I would have thought he had used on Scott when he was a little boy. Looking up at me, he begins, "Holland, this is Ranger." He stands, still petting the dog. "And, Ranger, this is Holland." The dog approaches me with his cold nose while I'm on my knees, and he's nudging me to pet him.

"Hey, boy." I caress his fur when Maguire puts his arm around Kat. I become irrationally angry. But it's not intimate. He's leading her to the car parked in front of the large garage on the other side of the big gravel driveway I somehow missed when we pulled up.

With Ranger on my heels, I open the door to his house, as Maguire says goodbye to Kat. I say good riddance. Sliding the front door open, I'm met with a house that screams Maguire Parrish. A couple feet from the door is a couch that sits perpendicular to the sliding front doors. A huge television sits in front of it. The sofa looks uncomfortable as hell, all contemporary. Behind the couch is the dining room table next to the kitchen. It's small, but a sizeable butcherblock island gives a definition between the kitchen and dining room space. The kitchen takes up the whole wall on the back part of the house, with open shelving holding all white dishes.

Back in the small living room, against the same wall as the kitchen, is a little desk where Scott and my wedding picture sits. And to finish up the open living space is his La-Z-Boy chair. It's one large rectangle that encompasses the living room, dining room, and kitchen. A hallway leads back from the dining room to one end of the house with another hallway that leads to the other end.

I'm attempting to guess where my room is when Maguire enters, with his duffle bag and one of my suitcases. "Fuck, I'm so happy to be home." He sees me in the middle of everything when he cocks his head to the left. "Your room is back here." The hallway from the living room is the road I should have taken and almost did. But now, I want to see what *his* room looks like. Is it as perfect for Maguire as the rest of his house?

He opens one of the three doors down at the end of the small hallway. "Here you go, darlin'."

The room is tiny, a full-size bed in the space with a long dresser and a single nightstand. "I wanted something that's yours. I had Ned's wife, Elise, pick out a new bedspread for you."

I like it, it's a purple paisley print. "She washed it along with the sheets. You can crawl into bed anytime. Kat brought us lasagna if you're hungry."

I turn, not sure what to say. "You mean, Kat, *your not-girlfriend*. She certainly didn't know I was coming."

His chin hits his chest and his hands rub his forehead. "Darlin', Kat and I have an arrangement. I don't date. Neither does she. I enjoy her company. We are what we need. Please don't make it something it's not. But at the same time, I don't like to fuck senseless women. It's not wrong what we have and somehow when you bring it up, it seems *very, very wrong*." He turns, walking away from me. "So, I'm getting myself some of her food. You can go to bed or you can join me. The choice is yours."

CHAPTER 15

H ow does this little girl get under my skin so easily? And Kat—showing up like she had. For a second, I thought she'd get her hackles up, but she didn't. She only hugged me, whispering in my ear all she could do to make me feel better. Yeah, I can't say when I've been jacking off the last couple of weeks, she's the face I see.

Kat will always be special to me, even if she's the woman I sleep with, too. I open up the oven where she left our dinner. I'm excited to be eating a home-cooked meal after all these weeks of consuming most of my breakfasts, lunches, and dinners at every diner from North Carolina to here.

But as I settle in, grabbing a plate from the open shelves, the presence of Scott in my house is all around me. The memories are closing in like my home is shrinking by the second. On the fridge is a picture he sent of Mark and him overseas on one of his tours. I have an old photo of him in a soccer uniform I've kept out since he was ten, at my eye level. It's faded though I still see the same toothy grin which has greeted me every morning when I grab cream for my coffee.

A coat rack sits at the front door, and I turn to see his Tarheels cap he'd forgotten when he visited a couple months ago. Man, for a kid from Virginia, he could have bled Carolina blue. It was imprinted in his soul. He'd watch every basketball game as if he was playing in it himself.

I walk over, ignoring the lasagna that had been the beacon at first to bring me in the kitchen. I pull off the hat, where Scott left it. I smell it—it still has his aroma. I turn to see Holland and his wedding picture on the desk on the same wall as the kitchen. It sits next to a framed picture of his handprints he made for me before Christine moved him to Virginia. Like the soccer picture, it's faded, but his little hand reminds me of all the times when he was small, he'd reach out and hold my hand to say, *"I love you, Daddy. I hope I grow big and strong like you."* Remembering those words in my mind, I sit down at the desk, holding his picture—looking at it like the lifeline it now is to the memories I have of my son.

I stand, grabbing the lasagna from the stove to place it quickly in the fridge. I can't eat, not now. I go back to the picture of his hand, pull it toward me, and hug it to my body. I don't stop until I get to my bedroom where I sit and cry for the son I'll never hold or hug again.

After ten minutes of pouting in my room, I owe Maguire an apology. He's right. It's consensual. Why have I allowed my panties to get in a bunch over it? I know the answer to that question but hell on a sticky bun, I can't admit it out loud.

In the open living space encompassing the den, dining room, and kitchen, I don't see Maguire. The oven is empty. The lasagna is uncovered in the fridge. I rummage through the drawers to get some tin foil to cover it. Behind the kitchen on the complete opposite end of the house from my room, I hear a muffled noise. I can't make it out, not at first. But nosy as I am, I walk toward his door. It takes me a minute. He's crying. Something about Scott, from the pictures of him on the fridge to the other memories he has of him in this house, must have become too real to him at this moment.

I stand still. Should I knock? Go to him to be his comfort? Let him hold me as we grieve together. I can't— for so many reasons I won't try to articulate. I slide down the wall next to his room. Memories assault me of my last conversation with my husband. It was a Skype call.

"Hell, Holland, I miss you so much." *I've been crying ten minutes before he called, missing him though I'd just seen him a couple weeks before. "Holly, honey, have you been crying?" he asks.*

"Yeah," I begin, I can never keep anything from him. "I just miss your strong arms keeping me safe."

He winks at me. "I know, hon." Emotions make him uncomfortable and he always shies away from them, because he doesn't know how to comfort me from afar. He gets a smile on his face. I know where this is leading. "Want to hear a joke, Holly?"

I smile because this is my man, my jokester, and I love him so much. And his jokes are sure to make me laugh because they are always dirty. "Sure, hit me," I begin.

"What's the difference between a tire and three hundred and sixty-five used condoms?" he asks, his

eyebrows raised.

I take the bait, "I have no idea, babe."

He begins to laugh before he delivers the punch line. "One's a Goodyear. The other's a great year." We both erupt in loud laughter. We talk for another ten minutes, nothing exceedingly memorable, but I'll always have that last laugh to help me to remember the good times.

Maguire's cries intensify. I know he needs his space, to truly get them out. He'll put on a brave face for me, so I stand quietly and head back to my room where I'm sure to do the same thing—grieving for the loss I'm confident I'll never get over.

CHAPTER 16

Maguire

I wake up to Ranger's nose on my own. The sun is shining through a couple of blinds that aren't turned the correct way. I don't remember falling asleep and I'm still in my jeans from yesterday. The breakdowns that come over me too quickly have so many emotions I can't explain. I've never sifted through all the feelings that converge on me quickly. Not when I caught Christine in bed with another guy or when she took Scott away. It's a sensation I'm unable to put into words. And receiving sympathy from anyone makes it ten times worse. I'm not one who wears my emotions on my sleeve. My mind silently reminds me that I'm still in this world where my son no longer exists.

I push my sheets back while Ranger jumps off the bed. How in the world did he not only get back into the house, let alone in my room? But I've missed my furry friend. "Boy, you need to go out?" I somehow had shed my t-shirt, opening the door to brewed coffee. I'm out of my element and have lost my bearings when I round the corner to the kitchen, running smack dab into someone. Oh, shit, for a split second I'd forgotten I'm now sharing my house with another person.

"Ah, crappity crap—you scared me." Holland's voice is loud, louder than she typically is in the morning.

When she backs up, she looks up and down. It's now I realize I have no shirt on. Above my heart is the word Scott with his date of birth. Her eyes fixate on it, my son's name etched in my skin.

"Wow, I had no idea." She reaches for Scott's name and immediately drops her hand. "How long have you had it?"

I worm around her, attempting to get away from her gaze. "Um, I got it the day Christine left for Virginia when Scott was six." The loss of him that day had always been what I compared loss to until Christine called me with the news over a month ago.

"I've been thinking of getting a tattoo, too, for Scott, where I can carry him around with me everywhere."

My back is to her, Ranger at my feet ready for me to let him out. Holland is getting closer to me, as I'm desperate to have space between us without a shirt.

"Wanna go out, boy?" I ask my dog, walking to the back door. And with how loud my daughter-in-law walks, she's close on my heels. "That's not a bad idea," I mention, about the tattoo. I'm on my way back to my room and she's still fucking following me.

"Maybe we can go today?" Why does she have to be so loud when it's just her and me in the house, but for once, it's not the loudness of her voice, it's her words.

"Darlin', you can't get a tattoo now." I twist my body as I stand in front of my bedroom door. Her hands are on her hips. Shit, I have got to get some clothes on. But as I watch her, pissing me off a little with her absurd, *let me get a tattoo while I'm pregnant,'* kind of claim, she's also as cute as ever. I'm trying to make the wood of my cock calm down a bit.

"Why can't I get a tattoo?" she asks.

I point to her belly as I turn around and she begins to follow me as I cross the threshold to my bedroom. I turn as her foot is about to step over it. "Um, darlin', can you give me a second?" I shut the door pretty much in her face, but I need a moment to calm the fuck down. As soon as I relax, my fucking boner sprouts to life and I'm relieved it's just me. Fuck, I need to get laid, to get her out of my system.

I leave Holland to her thoughts for a while as I get into the shower. Shit, I need to jack off, but if I do, I'll be jacking off to the images of Holland.

Holland is sitting on the couch. It's faced away from my bedroom and all I can see are the purple strands falling over it. She must hear the creak of my door and she twists her body around. I've taken thirty minutes for me and now I'm showered and shaved. Grabbing for my own keys I've not used in a month, I make my way to the sliding front door, pulling at my UCLA ballcap that's right next to Scott's Heels hat.

"Darlin', I've got an errand to run. I'll be back shortly."

She stands. "Wait, can I come? I don't want to be left alone here on my first day."

Ranger scratching at the front door directs my attention to him, and not Holland.

"Sorry, I need some time to myself—a little breather, going to see Ned and chat about some business stuff. I'll be back soon and then I'm yours the rest of the day." Well, shit, what am I saying?

She sits back down, her phone in her hands. "Um, okay." Her voice goes quiet and I don't miss her disappointment.

I let Ranger in and he moves over to Holland. He jumps on the couch, laying his head on her lap. "Well, aren't you the sweetest eighty-pound lap dog," Holland says as I shut the door.

I knock on her door lightly. I'm not sure I want to be here. But I need something to get Holland out of my system. I'm a dick, using her like this, but it's what we do. Use each other for this need—this desire.

She opens the door. I have no idea if her daughter is at her dad's this weekend. We don't involve our kids, that's not how this works. She pulls it back, just enough to see me when a broad grin covers her face.

Kat is beautiful. She's appropriately aged for me at thirty-seven. Her ex-husband's extracurricular duties included him sharing his seed with the greater Northern California population like a cat in heat.

Kat's light blonde hair falls over her shoulders. Her almost gray eyes sparkle. Could I have loved Kat? Possibly if we hadn't been screwed up by each other's exes. Her divorce is much more recent, where the travesties of Christine continue to haunt me, especially now.

I don't say anything, but push her up against the wall. "Is Adeline here?" I ask.

Her lips have already found their way to my neck, peppering kisses down it. "No, at her dad's." She's multitasking, unbuttoning my pants, pulling them down just a bit as her hand wraps around my shaft. "Shit, M, I've missed you." It's what Christine called me all those years ago. I didn't put a stop to it because Kat is different than Christine. It helps me to remember I can't lump all women into the Christine category.

Pulling at her arms, I push them roughly above her head. "Yes, you know how I like it." I look into her eyes and still.

I expect to see the deep dark brown color, not the gray of Kat's. She's staring at me. This is a good woman. But all I can think about as I look at her hair falling right above her tits is what it would look like with purple ends. "Shit, Kat," I say, buttoning up my pants, "I'm sorry, I just can't right now." I don't wait for a reply; I only turn around and jet out. Fuck, I'm such a prick.

I'm at the lake on my property, but instead of taking the road that leads to my house and then the service road that heads out to the lake, I make my way around, avoiding my home. Avoiding my daughter-in-law. I look at my phone and my heart falls.

I step outside and stare at the calm waters housing many residents. I opted to have my house built away from the lake, giving me the seclusion I need. I didn't want speed boats flying by my house with jet skis. But to be near the water, a half of a mile had been the cherry on the top. I have a little dock and my boat here. But for now, I sit on the top of my own pickup truck to think when a text comes through.

Kat: I can't imagine what you're going through, M. I'm here. Just know this.

She thinks I bolted because I miss my son. *I do miss*

my son. But it's not why I ran. I couldn't have sex with her when another person's face is floating through my mind.

"Maguire." Her loud but sweet voice pulls me out of my daydreams. "What are you doing here?"

She has Ranger on a leash. The traitor seems to have found another human he may like more than me. I stay propped on the hood of my Tundra. "Just thinking. I come here when I need some perspective."

"Yeah, I can see why. I had no idea where your dog was taking me until I rounded the corner and saw you." She stands in front of me and points to the part of the hood I'm not sitting on. "Do you mind?"

I reach for her hand when she puts one foot on my bumper, and I haul her up. With the wind blowing, I catch a faint hint of sandalwood, which is odd on a girl. And as much time as I've spent with her, her scent changes from day to day as does her crazy clothes. She's back to wearing a large ass white men's t-shirt, a pair of neon green leggings with silver hearts speckled throughout and pink Converse shoes.

"Did you get a chance to see Ned?" she asks.

I shake my head back and forth. "No, never made it that far." She can't see my eyes; they're covered by my aviators.

"Shitake mushroom, this sunlight," she begins, not asking me if I've been anywhere.

I pull my aviators from my face, bringing the bill of my cap down. "Here, use these." She smiles, putting my sunglasses on. "Do you need to go anywhere? Maybe get some food for the house. Specific things you like? I mean, Kat got the bare necessities."

At the mention of Kat, she turns her head, "Look, about Kat, I was a bitch yesterday. It's hard to understand your relationship with her, especially since I miss my husband so fuc—I mean, freaking much. But you're right, you're an adult, hurting no one. If she brings you comfort, then go do what you do."

I don't want to talk about this, not any longer, especially after what had happened today. "Um, thanks." I leave it at that. "So, want to go to the grocery store later?" I suggest.

"Sure, but if you don't mind, I'd like to just sit here for a while."

Her stare has not left the lake. *My stare* doesn't leave her profile. "Sure, darlin', whatever you'd like."

I don't know what provokes me to bring this up. Silence doesn't bother me when I'm around Maguire, but I blurt it out anyway. "Did you know Scott loved to tell dirty jokes? I mean, nothing about our sex life, but just funny one-liners. He normally left me with one every time we spoke."

I think when I said dirty jokes, he jolted his head around so fast he almost fell off the truck. But with him no longer in glasses, the second I talk about our sex life, he starts coughing. When he's finally calm and can breathe again, he looks at me, giggling like a girl.

"Well, you certainly have my attention." He stops for a brief second as if he has something to say and then continues, "And no, I didn't know this little fact about my son. But I'd love to hear one—maybe your favorite."

I think long and hard. There were so many. A lot were meant to get me horny so I could tell him what I'd do to him if he were home. I leave this little fact out of the story.

I think for a second and then a classic pops in my mind. "What did the hurricane say to the coconut tree?"

He squints his eyes at me and chuckles. "Hell, I have no idea, but I'm bracing myself for this one."

I know it's odd, what I'm about to say to my father-in-law of all people, but I'm going to be living with this man. I need to become comfortable with him. I smile when I reply, "Hold on to your nuts, this ain't no ordinary blowjob."

He almost falls off the truck while his hysterical laughs fill the air. "Hell, not many women would mention the word blowjob in front of their father-in-law."

"I don't shy away from what I want to say if you haven't noticed." I'm still laughing at Maguire, who is honestly funnier than the joke was.

"Yeah, Holland, I've noticed. Never a boring moment with you."

My head turns to stare at him, though my eyes are covered by his aviators. He can't see me watching him when he brings his hand to my chin. He doesn't pull away, not like before.

"It's safe to say there's no one quite like you, darlin'."

I don't *pull away* either. I should. I need to. Maguire's touch, it's so familiar yet so forbidden and desired. "You call everyone darlin'?" I ask. In his pet name, it's still so taboo due in part to what the six-letter word does to me. My skin flushes and my knees become weak with his own little term of endearment.

His face changes and he fixates on his hand touching me. He pulls it away like I'm fire to his touch. But his gaze, it's just as intent. "No, you're it. Never called anyone this before. Just you."

"Why?" My desire to know what makes this man tick

is all I want in the here and now. Do I care for him, needing his touch on me, because he's an older version of Scott or his own man?

"I don't know. The day I saw you walk in, your purple hair, the brightness of your clothes. You'd always been so precious to Scott. I know he called you Holly. I suppose it came out naturally, my own understanding of what you are. To me, you are as darling as they come."

His hand lands on my cheek again, brushing it with his thumb. As quick as it's on me, it's gone immediately. He pushes himself off the top of his truck. "Listen, Holland, I have an idea. Ned has all the contractors lined up. Until then, let's go to my warehouse. I have some custom furniture. I'll let you pick out what you want."

Maguire makes beautiful custom furniture. He'll make ten to fifteen of the same item by hand and sell them for thousands of dollars. I'm about to protest. I can't let him spend this money on me. He turns around and I'm still on the hood of the truck. He walks in front of me and grabs at my waist, bringing my body down.

"Don't argue with me," he commands, quickly dropping his touch from mine.

"I don't need anything fancy," I begin.

"It's what I do. Everything in my house, from my cabinets to my table to my bed. Even the bathroom, I built everything. Of course, any apartment of mine will have the same feel."

He passes me on his way to his side of the truck. Climbing in as Ranger jumps into the bed of his vehicle, it occurs to me. "You do a lot of building at home in the garage below. Scott said you build at night."

"Oh, yeah, I thought of that. I won't be building in there once you move into your new apartment. I have had plans for an actual building to be built near the garage. Contractors are coming out to start pouring the concrete. The construction will be done before the baby comes." He pauses at the mention of his grandchild. "By the way, I want you to pick out some options for wood for the baby's room. I'll build the crib, changing table, and dresser and anything else he or she needs." He stops. "The bedroom for the baby won't be super big, but he or she will have their own space. *You will have your own space.*"

We stop by the house where Ranger jumps from the back of the truck and lies in the shade under the canopy on the front porch.

He yells out to his dog, "Guard the house, Ranger. I'm counting on you."

I giggle—I'm positive Ranger would only lick someone to death, if anything.

As he's slowing down for all the potholes that lead down the road from his property, I startle him when I reach for his hand. "Everything you're doing for me, Sarge, it's outside of the realm of your promise, you know this, right? Scott only asked you to make sure I had a job and a place my parents wouldn't worm their way into my life, dragging me down with them."

He brakes immediately. "Darlin', I'm not doing enough to honor my son, believe me." My hand is still in his. "If you only knew."

It's the first time he admits what I've already suspected, but it reaffirms I've not been off base.

"Maguire." I don't move my hand from his. I can't.

His own hand reaches for my cheek again. "You know?" he asks. It's like we can't say it, verbally announcing what this is between us because it makes it that more real and forbidden.

"You know, too?" A tear falls from my face.

In the middle of this small dirt road, I ready myself for this kiss, it's coming and coming quickly. Until we hear a loud turbo engine coming our way. We break from one another as if what could have happened would never happen ever again.

CHAPTER 17

Maguire

I'm saved with the roar of my best friend's truck barreling up the long road to my property. Her gaze is on the outside. Her shoulders stiffen and she won't turn toward me, I know our moment has passed. And thank fuck.

I don't utter a word to Holland when I open the door as Ned approaches me. This man, not only my business partner, is my mentor and best friend. He's only ten years my senior, but this guy doesn't look it. He's not as big as me, but when the man hugs, he does it with his whole body.

He left me in North Carolina several weeks ago, escorting me on the plane there. I'd not been in any shape to take care of the travel arrangements on my own. He was with me for a week, being my rock, before he had to return. Plus, he's single-handedly been in charge of the apartment for Holland.

I'm a man's man, always have been, but when it comes to this big teddy bear, he sees the real me.

"Fuck, man, I'm so happy to have you home," Ned begins. I look up, his sweet wife of twenty years is in their cab, tears falling down her face, too, at the sight of me. With everything and everyone I had to be strong for, I lose it in his arms—especially after what almost happened with Holland.

After a minute of crying and Ned being my anchor, I look back at him. "Well, shit, what a pussy thing to do."

"Hell, Maguire, don't insult me like this. You need to cry, to hit someone, someone to throw back beers with, yell at and at the end of the day, need to cry again, I'm your fucking man—you get me?"

Ned's words pierce my heart, not because they hurt, but I've been strong for everyone else, knowing he's my person gives me a much-needed source of comfort. "Yeah, you son of a bitch," I joke, my term of endearment for him to lighten the mood a bit. "We're heading to the warehouse. I'm letting Holland pick out some items for her apartment. Want to meet us there?" With a nod and agreement, I sulk over to my truck.

Back in the cab, Holland is still turned to the side. What can I say, *Sorry for almost taking advantage of you? Sorry for nearly kissing my son's wife?* No, there's nothing to say and for this reason, I back up a little to give Ned room to turn around and I follow him in silence.

Our warehouse and corporate offices are on the outskirts of town. This town isn't all that big to begin with. Coral Creek, sitting at about three thousand in population gives off the hometown feel I love. Plus, I live far enough on the outskirts to enjoy the peace and quiet of it all. Holland has been plastered to the window since we left. Every once in a while, I see her out of the corner of my eye, wiping her face.

I'm such a dick. First today with Kat and now with

Holland. I've never been this off-kilter before. One could say it's losing Scott. Sure, I could use his death as an excuse, but deep down, I know it's more.

It's the biggest reason I need to get the apartment finished. Holland in my house is going to be a temptation I can't deny much longer.

Once in the warehouse, and with Ned's wife doting on Holland, he takes me aside to our offices.

"Shit," I start, seeing my workspace for the first time since that fateful day. "I've missed this place, Ned. And your ugly mug."

I grab for a bottle of the best Canadian whisky from my bottom drawer and pour us a drink. Passing it over to Ned on the other side of my desk, he holds it, his lips pursed. This is when I know he has something to say. "Out with it, Ned. I've known you long enough."

"Holland, she's certainly quiet."

Could he read it? Could he sense it with the way my eyes roam over her tiny body? Or how I want to fist her hair in my hand. Does he know me this well?

With a long pull of my whisky, I shrug a non-committal answer. "Yeah, she hurts. It's deep within her. Hell, it's deep for all of us."

"Have you talked to Christine? She's up in arms over Holland living here." My eyes dart to his. I should have known.

Once, a long time ago, Christine and Elise were the best of friends. We all were. When she cheated on me and punished me by moving Scott across the country, Elise distanced herself. But the sweet nature in Elise would not have left Christine alone. She reached out to her. I'm not surprised. Elise had finished chemo a month before Scott was killed. She wasn't strong enough to fly out for the funeral. Though, she has been a comfort to Christine through many phone calls.

"Oh, poor Elise. She has to hear all Chris's rants, doesn't she?" I ask and a nod of his head gives me the answer. "And what's her opinion?"

He shakes his head at me. "You know Elise. She'll love on anyone who needs her, whether it's the bitch known as your ex-wife or your daughter-in-law. I bet she's already making plans for Holland in some way, shape, or form." He props his elbows onto the front of my desk, placing his whisky down. "But, Maguire, it's you I'm worried about."

"I miss my son." It's the truth. I can't go any deeper, not now. After my breakdown last night and the events of my day, my emotion meter is tapped out. I stand, returning my alcohol to the bottom cabinet. With Ned leading the way, we find the girls down in the warehouse. And I'm right as rain. Elise is in the middle of everything, pulling out cabinets and other furniture, chatting with Holland as if they are old friends. With Elise Landon and her mother hen ways, I have no doubt they will be.

In Maguire's surplus, I'm drawn to a grayish color of reclaimed wood. I walk over to it while Elise and Ned discuss finishes in my apartment. I don't know why I'm drawn to this wood. I'm not one for super modern furniture as are the vibes of this timber. I touch it, it's smooth. The more my eyes fixate on it, the more I know this is the type of crib I want for my baby.

I've been trying to keep my distance from Maguire.

I had been so close to kissing him. H...E...double toothpicks. How had I allowed myself to even think it—let alone almost do it?

"Darlin'," he whispers behind me and I twist around.

"You scared the beetle juice out of me." He cocks his head to the side as he begins to laugh so hard, it becomes soundless and his chuckle is quiet. My odd words confuse him, but in his grin, he's also amused. This is the first time in a while his smile reaches the greenish hazel hues of his eyes. And it's cute. No, it's sexy.

He skips over the fact that he legit scared the crap out of me when his eyes search the same gray grain in the wood that has caught my attention. "Do you like this?" he asks.

"Yeah, there's something about it. I'm not sure if it's the right kind of wood, but do you think it would work for a..." I stop and bring my loud ass mouth down a decibel or five when I whisper, "Could it work for a crib?"

With his expertise, he must know. "Yeah, this will do fine. It's a beautiful wood. I'll get Ned to help me load it. I'll want to work with it first before I make a..." He lowers his voice, too, and says the next words so quiet I almost don't hear. "I want to build some things to test the durability because if it's going to sleep my grandbaby, it will be safe as fuck."

He's opened the door and I grin when I ask, "How, in pray tell, is fuck safe?"

He twists his mouth to one side, as he does when he's annoyed. "Holland," he croons.

"Maguire," I respond in a snarky kid-like tone.

I walk away laughing because nothing seems to give me more joy than goading my father-in-law.

CHAPTER 18

Three days. It's been the number I've purposely avoided Maguire around the house. I'm up early for some unknown reason. An internet article claims insomnia during pregnancy isn't uncommon. It's funny how one moment I can barely make it to my room before I'm out like a light and the next, I'm wide awake counting sheep.

I'm a sucker for old movies. AMC is playing *A Street Car Named Desire*. I'm watching Marlon Brando tossing Vivien Leigh's suitcase when a reflection from the television screen scares me. "Fiddlesticks, Maguire, you scared the shitake mushrooms out of me."

Shaking his head at my words, his attention is on the screen when, out of nowhere, he bellows, "Stelllllla!"

It makes me smile—*no, he makes me smile*. It's not original—not in the least, but it's still funny. He takes a seat in his chair, kitty-corner from the couch. "You know what? If Scott was a girl, I wanted to name him Stella, strictly based on my love for this movie."

I'm on the opposite end of the sofa. It's as if Maguire purposely tries to put as much physical space as humanly possible between the two of us. "Are you a Marlon Brando fan?" I ask.

"I love all old movies. Besides a good football game or college basketball, I almost always watch an old classic."

Who knew? "I would have never guessed this about you." I stand before my yearning for physical affection finds its way to my father-in-law. I fake a yawn, though it's now believable, at three in the morning or as Scott always called it—the devil's hour.

"Going back to bed?" he asks, and his head follows every move I make with his question.

"Yeah, it's late." I start down the hallway, looking forward now, not back at him as I'd been doing.

"It sure is," he calls behind me. "It's the devil's hour, you know." I stop at his words. His comment and his phrase only further cement the fact I care for this man because he's the carbon copy of my husband. I take one step and command myself to continue toward my bedroom.

The Sunday night before I'm due to start my new job, I walk down the hall from my bedroom, where I hide most of the time when Maguire's in the house. He's in the kitchen, making something, beckoning my hungry body out of seclusion.

"Hey, stranger," Maguire begins, looking straight at me.

"Oh, hey. I think I may be feeling better. Whatever you're making smells amazing. Is there enough for me?" I raise one eyebrow at him, physically inhaling the aroma in the kitchen.

A slow smile builds when his eyes make firm contact with mine. "Of course, darlin'. Glad to see you looking a bit better." He reaches up to his open shelves, grabbing two plates. When he does this, his shirt rides up and I see a hint of his abs. I've seen him shirtless a couple of times and hell, he's simply beautiful.

"I've made a chicken pot pie," he explains, though it's as obvious as his handsome face.

I cross over to the kitchen and sneak around him, moving to the refrigerator. I'm so thirsty for orange juice. Opening it up, I'm relieved to see the O.J. is still there. Pregnancy cravings are no joke. I watch Maguire cut the pie meticulously as though he's using a saw on something he's about to build. I stop with the O.J. in the air, ready for me to pour it, staring at his detailed cutting skills.

"Holland, why are you staring at me so intensely?" he asks, a little of his dry humor in his tone.

"I've never seen someone cut a chicken pot pie with such precision." Placing the spatula between the crust of the pie and the round pan, he tugs at the piece carefully, bringing it up in a perfect triangle. He neatly positions it on the plate and begins with the second piece. After witnessing the perfectionist he is, I finish pouring my juice and grab my serving, moving to the kitchen table.

I wager to guess Maguire eats all his meals in front of the television, watching ESPN. But he says nothing to me, pouring some milk, and bringing his dinner to the table.

One bite of the hot creamy goodness and I'm almost moaning. I have forgotten what real food tastes like. I've been living on Lemonheads, saltines, and ginger ale. My second bite brings me more pleasure and I stop when I sense Maguire's gaze on me.

"What?" I ask with my mouth full of this dish.

"Wow, darlin', never seen someone get so into their food."

I've not thought what my moans actually might mimic. My face flushes and he chuckles, his deep snicker causing my stomach to tighten like it does when an orgasm is so very close.

"I'm just so fucking happy to see you eating. I was getting a little worried."

I'm thankful he changes the subject from my questionable moans. Continuing to shovel his meal into my mouth, he puts down his fork, steepling his fingers at his chin.

"So, I've been thinking." Oh, lord, this can't be good, I silently say to myself. "You don't need to start work tomorrow. You can wait until the baby comes. Or you can begin college right away."

With food in my mouth, I don't wait to voice my disbelief at first. I push myself back slightly, increasing my own personal space. "What? I need money, Maguire. I can't live off of you. I need food, gas, tuition, stuff for the baby, childcare, a new car." I swallow the rest of my food and take a quick drink of my juice. "I may be young, but I know enough about a budget to comprehend I need it. And as a matter of fact, I can make a dollar stretch." My voice seems a little less rattled than I am.

He places his hands on the table, his body stiffening. "Holland," he begins, scrubbing the scruff of his beard. In it, I can really see his gray.

There's this way he forcefully says my name, lowering his timbre a bit when his entire face reddens. It was how I knew I pushed Scott, too. "I'm not trying to control you. I'm only worried about the pregnancy. You'll be working in a warehouse."

"Has anyone else ever worked for you during their pregnancy?" I ask.

He rolls his eyes. "Of course, but none of those people have been my daughter-in-law, carrying my late son's child. So, please excuse the over-protectiveness I have concerning you and my grandbaby."

I push my food aside. I've lost my appetite. "So, it's about the baby only?" I ask, tossing the napkin which had been on my lap.

"You are so fucking stubborn. Of course, it's not just about the baby. But I think I can honestly say that your baby, Scott's and yours is the only thing getting you through his death. And if something were to happen, I can't stand by watching you hurt again. Shit, Holland, can't you see this?"

I lean my head back, looking at the ceiling to take a second to think. "And what, pray tell, would I do for money? I'm not living off of Scott's insurance. Now, with the baby, I'll need to set aside a little for him or her."

This time, he rubs his forehead, taking in a deep breath. "I have set aside money for Scott since he was six. It had been meant to help with college or go toward his partnership with Ned and me. Or to buy a house. It's Scott's, so it rightfully belongs to you. I'd not brought it up yet because you're so hung up on paying me back and not wanting a handout, I decided to tackle this issue today because *now* it's necessary."

I scoot my chair close to Maguire, a smile meeting his sullen scowl. "I appreciate it. And since it's truly Scott's, maybe you can give it to the baby, for his or her future. But I want to work. I'm looking forward to it for many reasons. I promise you though, if work or anything I'm doing puts this baby in danger, I'll stop and will reconsider your offer to dip into Scott's savings. How about this for a compromise, Sarge?" I impart.

I'm met with a small smile and my appetite returns. Pulling the plate toward me and disposing of the napkin on my dinner, I take another bite as we both eat in peace and quiet.

I have a half a dozen towels in my hands, passing Holland in the living room, on my way to her bathroom. I've been a stickler about having everything organized for the week ahead of me. When I start a new project—my heart and soul know nothing else until I'm done. And I'm ready to pour everything into my next design; a fifteen-piece series of headboards. With the reclaimed wood I've been hoarding, just for a project like this, I have my design locked in my mind, ready for it to become a reality.

In the bathroom Holland has taken over, I'm face-to-face with the many reasons she smells different every day. On the small shelf at the bottom of the mirror sits at least fifteen different lotions and perfumes. Underneath the mirror sits fifteen or so more. To the side of the mirror, on another shelf I have hung up, lay a good thirty bottles.

I shake my head, returning to the living room where Holland is binge watching some sort of new adult drama she calls *The Bold Type*. Her focus is on the show and when I try to drag her attention to me, she doesn't flinch. "Holland, darlin'," I say, blocking her view to the T.V.

"*Um, sure, Sarge,* I'm not watching this, go ahead." Her sarcasm drips from her sweet lips.

"Okay, smart ass, just pause the show for a second." I sit on the chair and I always do this to stay as far away from her as I can. "So, what is up with the sixty plus bottles of perfume and lotions?"

Adjusting in the couch, moving her legs under her ass, a giant mind-blowing smirk makes it almost impossible to breathe. With her little laugh, she affects my body more than any woman ever has.

"Only sixty. Wow, that's a small percentage of what I own. What can I say, I can't choose one scent I like." She moves her entire body toward me. "See, I have this thing with Bath and Body Works."

I don't know this store, why would I? If it's about perfumes and smell-good items, I'm at a loss for words. I've never bothered myself in spoiling another female, not since Christine.

"See," she continues. "Every deployment, birthday, holiday, and just because he wanted, Scott would get me an entire set of new aromas. He knew it was my guilty pleasure. Some women have a thing for shoes, or purses, or designer jeans. Mine is lotions and perfumes."

Every layer of Holland she reveals to me only makes me want to get to the next layer. She returns her eyes back to the television. I don't take my eyes off of her. It's then, I have a keen awareness of my own heartbeat and I'm flooded with warmth for this girl in front of me. I call her a girl to keep my desires in check but as I watch her, the curves of her hips, even sitting down and the cleavage revealed by her tight white tank top tells me there's nothing kid-like about this woman in front of me.

Turning her head quickly, I avert my gaze away. The last thing I need is her catching me spying on her. I stand, giving her a gentle smile and return to my bedroom. I'm out of my element here. Yet, all I can continue to think about is what her nipples would taste like. I fall back on my bed—frustrated in more ways than one.

CHAPTER 19

If losing a child isn't awful enough, the pity and whispers of others are fucking brutal. The second I stride into the front offices, ready to get back to a semblance of normal, everyone stops to stare. It doesn't help I have *the widow* with me. To make matters worse, the area which leads to my office is filled with the entire staff, administration and faculty for an all-hands meeting I'm apparently skipping. Making my way up the steps to my office, I can feel everyone's gaze on me. An empty sensation in my gut takes over and I want to be anywhere but here. Scraping my fingers through my hair with one hand and rubbing the back of my head with the other, I watch Holland, who won't make eye contact with me.

Odd laughter I've not yet heard from my daughter-in-law fills the office once we enter it and close the door. She begins, "Well, that was awkward as fuck."

I don't bother to remind her how much I loathe this one particular word forming on her lips. She usually does it more to annoy me, but when she's nervous, it slips out.

"They all loved Scottie. It's their loss, too, and they don't know how to react."

She sits straight up in her chair. She can't take one more *I'm sorry for your loss* sentiment when she begins, "So, tell me about your company." Her tone and pitch are completely changed from before. This is a subject, unlike her loss, she wants to talk about. Her lips turn upward, and I smile whenever she does. She's that infectious.

"Well, this business started nineteen years ago." She shifts in her seat. "I was still married to Christine. She and Elise were the best of friends. Anyway, I'd been working as a carpenter barely making ends meet. Ned came out to our house one day with Elise. He and I were acquaintances. Christine invited them to stay for dinner and he admired our dining room table." Holland doesn't break eye contact with me. Actually, she scoots a bit closer, sitting across from my desk, like I'm about to give away the plot to one of her favorite new adult dramas she watches. "Christine went on and on about my skills. I took him out to my workshop where I'd housed a good portion of my inventory. At the time, the internet wasn't what it is now. But it was beginning to get big. He told me I could make good money. He started on a business plan. Ned acted as if he had no skills with woodworking whatsoever. After a year, he started building, and we branded out our business as hand-built furniture with limited inventory. From a business standpoint, we do custom builds by request, but the majority of our income originates from our limited catalog."

I don't know why she's watching me so intently, but it's adorable. "We found people loved the fact that our furniture was not mass produced and not built on an assembly line." I stop to ask, "Surely Scott had shared this with you?"

"He told me a little. But even if he had shared everything with me, I'd still want to hear it from you."

My eyes narrow in on her. "Why?"

"Do you know how much passion fills you when you talk about this? It's not just your job, it's your calling. Not everyone can say they do what they love. You can. For this very reason, I could listen to you all day long, chatting about this."

I pause at her compliment. "Wow, no one has ever said this to me before." I'm falling for my son's girl—she makes me a better person. I don't allow myself long to dwell on this when I begin again. "We devised a plan. I'd make a limited number of designs, all handcrafted. After the last one is sold, the design is retired. The less amount of product means there's more demand. I find fifteen is the lucky number. Now throughout the years, I have brought in a team of skilled carpenters who handcraft what I design. Their pieces will have their design number on the individual item. Customers are loyal to their builder and will order custom furniture from them. It's one way my carpenters can make a little more money on the side. But it's never on an assembly line. When so much furniture is mass produced from plywood, we only offer solid wood."

She's smiling at me. There are very few people who sit and listen to my love for the business like she's doing. Scott loved to hear about my projects, but besides Ned and himself, I've had very few to share this part of me with.

Because she doesn't interrupt, I continue. "Our big price items are dining room tables. We make fifty percent of our profit alone on them. Kitchen cabinets are next and then bedframes. We ship all over the world. A couple of years ago, we brought in Diane to help with home décor, with the same idea. She retired from her job of thirty years with a name brand furniture retailer. She moved to the mountains but wasn't ready to be home all day with her husband." We both laugh in unison. "She's a couple of years from actually retiring for good this time. So, I want you two to collaborate. She will, in essence, be your boss. Our home décor division is already bringing in three percent of our annual income after only two years. Right before the..." What do I say, the death of my son? I pause and she looks away. "Anyway, right before I flew to North Carolina, we'd moved the design section to a completely different part of the building with the idea of expanding distribution. Right now, our home décor is only domestic. Due to your seamstress skills, you will work on textiles. As your schooling progresses, we'll work on you taking over for Diane. We contract an artist to distribute her work as part of the whole Parrish & Landon custom paintings with her studio off of the design division."

She leans forward, her elbows on her knees. "Wow, Maguire, I had no idea. This is truly impressive. Scott was always so proud of you. He told me once that if he could be as happy in his job as you were, he'd be complete. He would have *me*—the love of his life and a job he loved almost as much."

"How do you do it?" I ask, leaning back in my chair, my muscles tense.

"What?"

"You take away burdens I've not been able to voice yet, like my regret of not giving my business up to be with Scott. It has always given me the most doubt as a parent. I always assumed I'd been selfish because I didn't walk away from my company."

She pulls her hair up in a ponytail when she stands. "Like I said before, you were the reason I fell in love with Scott."

I choke on her words.

"Think about it, can you imagine I'd be able to have fallen in love with him if Christine had been the one to influence him? No, it's you that made him the man he was."

And it's then I realize she affectionately looks at me the way she does because of Scott, I'm the older version of him. Why does this hurt so much? I'm jealous of my late son. What kind of sick motherfucker am I?

The new design house, as it's called, is beautiful. It's large, with big windows allowing natural light to pour in from the outside. Large industrial sewing machines are in the corner of a vast space. I salivate. Hell, I may orgasm. They are beauties. Carpet wheels cover the whole right wall. In front of the sewing machines is a design desk with my name on it.

A woman with short black hair sits at another design table at the far end of the room. Setting down her pen, she rushes at me. "You must be Holland. I'm glad to have you here." She embraces me as if we know one another already. "Oh, honey, aren't you the cutest thing." She's not condescending, she's sincere.

My mouth opens, about to return a compliment when a loud, "Well, fuck—not having you on the floor anymore Di is going to suck balls."

It's brash, it's crude, and I giggle at the feminine voice bellowing through the design center. "Hell, another chick in the house." This tall girl around my age stands in front of me and grins. "Ah, you're pretty." She gives me a hug—then pulls back. "So, you were married to Scott

Parrish, I guess that means you're not a lesbian."

I twist around in the design space. Are there cameras recording this? Is this some sort of weird indoctrination? I turn back to both Diane and the tall young woman near me when the two of them start to laugh hysterically. I'm still staring at this tall and thin giant of a girl. She has on a shirt that reads, *Lesbian Strong*. This explains her question from earlier. The sawdust covering her jeans and shoes tells me she's one of the carpenters. Her teal green eyes are playful, a broad smirk covers her face. The long Ombre grayish blue hair falls well past her back. She's pretty, a girl any guy would love to have on his arm.

"Great—Teagan, you've rendered our newest employee speechless." Diane gives her a playful shove. "Um, Holland, this is our resident mad woman. You'll find she's a ray of sunshine if you can get past her forwardness and foul language."

"Ah, Di, there's never a dull moment with me around."

I watch the witty commentary between these two. I'm holding my own side because I can't stop laughing along with them.

"So tell me, pretty girl, you into ladies?"

I'm snorting at her. I don't even know how to respond.

"Teagan, you're lucky you work with all men. And that no one will ever report you for sexual harassment." With her belly laugh, Diane holds her hand out as if she's telling Teagan no more.

This giant, compared to my small frame, holds her hand out for me. "I'm Teagan, by the way, in case that was lost in this weird as fuck translation. So, you must be straight?"

I extend my hand to shake this comical woman's own hand in front of me. "I'm Holland. And yes, I'm straight as an arrow."

"Well, hell, that sucks. But I'm glad to have more woman power in this place, finally." Her demeanor changes quickly. "Seriously, Holland. I'm awkward as fuck. Didn't know how to tell you how fucking sorry I am for your loss. Scott was a great man and I respected him a shit ton."

I've been offered so many condolences, I don't know how to handle it anymore. I start to speak, and my voice cracks. I grin at her. "You know, Teagan, I'm so tired of people pitying me. You coming in here—being you—is what I needed."

Teagan puts her arm around me. "Good to know I could be of service. Now, about this whole straight thing—are you sure?" She's grinning at me.

"Positive."

"Well, then friends? What do you say?" she asks.

I don't think I'd have a choice with this chick anyway.

It's in small little everyday things I think I just may be okay. This is one of them.

The military sent the rest of my items to Scott's permanent address. This was always our plan, and Scott made sure to use his dad's house.

I hated taking a day off the first week at a new job, but I had no choice. Waiting outside the garage for the movers, the sound of kicked up gravel from the road pulls me out of my thoughts of my husband. Expecting the moving truck, I look up to see Elise Landon's Mercedes pull up next to me.

She's the mother hen sort of type. In a business of mostly men, Elise has made it her job to be a surrogate mom to all of the women working at the factory.

"I know, I know," she begins, her bright blue eyes narrowing in on me. "You can tell me to leave if you need to do this alone, I will. My feelings won't be hurt."

She's younger than Ned by about five years and the dark brown hair she has styled in a shoulder length inverted bob, tells me she's up on modern trends. Her skinny jeans and gray heeled booties only reaffirm this. Pushing her large Audrey Hepburn glasses up on her head, her sweet smile calms me. I've never had a motherly person to bond with.

As she approaches me, she continues, "And I figured you had to be tired of that grumpy man you drove cross-country with. Hell, Maguire is great, but he's so freakin' moody, like a woman on her period."

A smirk covers my face and she matches my same grin. She's hit the nail on the head. "Yeah, you're right about him." I stand as she crosses the space between us. I'm not used to the affection this group of people show. It's overbearing yet comforting at the same time. The second Elise is within arm's reach, she pulls me close, and into a hug.

"Sweetie, just know you don't have to do this alone. You've got people here, ready to help."

Did she know I've never had a maternal figure in my life? Not even my own mother? Had Maguire told her *my own parents* couldn't travel the six hours to their son-in-law's funeral?

I've had close friends that became my family in the military. There were Sarah and Mark—who still are this to me. But Elise is different, and I crave whatever kind of friendship we'll build in the future.

I'm so tired of tears streaming down my face. I have enough of them at night when I cry myself to sleep at so many dreams shattered. I weep for our baby who will never know his or her father. I cry for my loneliness, wanting and needing his physical connection. I grieve for the dreams we had made and for the fact I'm living them without him. I sob for Maguire who misses his son so deeply, I read it on his face each morning he tries to put a brave front on for me.

And honestly, I'm relieved to have someone with me. Receiving the rest of Scott's belongings has me teeter-tottering on both anxiety and panic. I hadn't slept last night, and my appearance resembles a hobo. I never wanted to do this alone. When Maguire offered, he'd seen too much of my vulnerability and it was only leading to what we both knew we couldn't be to one another.

"Wow, how did you know I didn't want to do this by myself?" I ask, with Elise in front of me, her hands on my shoulders.

"Because, sweetie, no one should have to do this by themselves. I mean, if you need to be alone to go through his things, I get it, but as they deliver it, seeing the last of his stuff, you should have someone with you." She turns back to her car for a moment. Coming back, she's holding a tray of drinks and a white bag. "And because everything is better with food, I brought you the world-famous Auntie Lou's apple fritters."

We'd passed Auntie Lou's bakery many times on the way to work. When I mentioned to the Sarge we should stop, his response was, *"I ate enough junk on the road."* I knew I'd not be trying it with Maguire.

"And because I've learned you're a tea drinker, I brought you chamomile tea." She hands it over to me and we both sit down chatting as if we've known each other for years.

An hour later, we're deep into conversation. "Yeah, Teagan, she's a character. Let me guess, she asked you if you were a lesbian?" Elise questions.

We're laughing so hard, as I recreate the scene of my first encounter with the eclectic Teagan Erons. "Yep, she sure did."

"She's a funny one, that's for sure." She's listing all the women, seven in total now including me, working for Ned and Maguire. "Besides yourself, Diane, and Teagan, there's Irene, the boys' secretary. Jolene works as the purchasing liaison, Mira is the new artist, and Debra is the computer guru. We gals have to stick together. I take everyone to lunch once a month. Plus, we do dinner or game nights, too."

My eyes widen at her declaration. I'm amazed by her love for people and the true giver she is. We're into a conversation about the antics of all the women in the group when a large truck comes barreling up the drive. My heart sinks when her hand squeezes mine. "I know your parents weren't the hands-on type. I know Christine better than most, she's a hard woman to love, believe me. But you don't have to do this alone anymore, sweetie."

My inner voice repeats the words over and over again, silently, I can't believe this. I've always wanted a mother figure. Who knows if Elise Landon will be this for me, only time will tell but right away, in her words and reassurance, I know this woman will be someone significant in my life.

I only want the movers to place the boxes and the few items of furniture at the bottom of the stairs near my to-be apartment. After Elise left, knowing I had to do this on my own, I opened a few boxes. It's all I could do.

Pulling at the box marked pictures, I open it slowly and our wedding album is the first item I see. I take it gently, soreness creeping up into my throat and lungs. My hands grip the sides of the album with such force, my way of making sure this keepsake I'm holding will not be damaged. I take it with me as I sit on the steps leading to my apartment. Opening the first page is our official picture as husband and wife. We'd kept the plans to ourselves. Scott was certain Christine would try to stop the wedding. He hadn't slept for days, being conflicted over sharing our upcoming nuptials with his dad—since he had not wanted his mother there. In the end, we had Sarah and Mark stand up for us.

My dress was simple. It was white lace, stopping above the knee. Scott had on a simple pair of jeans and a button-down baby blue shirt. Sarah snapped the picture with her cell phone, but the photo encompassed everything of the two of us. I'm looking up into Scott's eyes and his face is tilted down to mine. We're smiling—we were so happy. Actually happy doesn't cut it. No, we had our whole lives ahead of us.

I stand, placing the album down. I'm not aware of where I'm at in the garage. Only that I'm hyperventilating. My breathing is so labored, I'm barely able to catch my breath until strong arms reach around my waist.

The voice itself is calming. The one word which is pulling me out of my grief is, "Darlin'," and I know who it is. Safe doesn't begin to describe how I feel with his arms enveloping me. "I got you, darlin', just breathe."

With each command of his words, I take another

calming breath as he turns me around to look at him. He pulls me tight to his body as my breathing starts to regulate. And it's in his arms I can start living again.

CHAPTER 20

Two weeks living with this man—I know his routines. He wakes at five a.m., in the name of everything holy and good in this world. What's wrong with him? He runs past the lake and back, about three miles he claims. He makes himself the same thing every morning for breakfast— two fried eggs, three turkey sausage patties, and one piece of wheat toast with way too much butter for someone's heart. He's in his room for a good hour then returns to the living room and watches some sort of show on ESPN, filling the house with his woodsy pine-like aftershave. His attire changes from day to day only in the color of the shirt he wears but the man displays his fine ass in a pair of jeans in a way many can't manage.

I, on the other hand, wake when I wake and scramble around in the morning to shower and dress, leaving my room and bathroom in disarray. I grab a hot tea and yogurt, normally eating in Maguire's truck on the way to work.

At night, he retires to his workshop. The man is

obsessed with building, but as I've come to find out, it's his passion and I enjoy watching him.

I'm in the main house applying to a variety of online colleges, but I'm lonely. I decide to go in search of him, not like I have far to look.

After making a cup of coffee for him, I cross the gravel driveway, surveying the progress of his new workshop. It's not big, maybe four hundred square feet. It's coming along, with the frame newly constructed. Entering his workspace in the garage, he's deep in thought, staring at one piece of wood, like him and this inanimate object are about to chat with one another.

"What's so interesting?" I ask, pulling him from his deep thoughts.

"Oh, I'm just looking at my design with this type of wood." He twists around, grabbing the coffee out of my hands. "I tell you what, darlin'," he begins, taking a swig of his drink. "For someone who despises coffee as you say, you sure make a great cup."

"Well, what can I say," I curtsy. "It's my superpower." I look at the stairwell to the right of his shop that leads to my *soon-to-be* home. "How's the progress going?"

"Oh, are you in a hurry to move out?" He leans against a worktable when I sit down on a bench.

"I'm sure you're ready to have your space back. I mean, I'm untidy and you cook for me every night."

He stands like he may walk toward me but then leans back on the table. "Let's get one thing clear, I love having you in my space. I never thought I was lonely, but now I realize I have been, for so long. Having you around, knowing you're in the house, gives me hope, and a purpose. It's hard to explain, I'm not one to talk about my feelings and emotions, but your spirit livens everything up."

We're getting bolder with one another. We're certainly more comfortable with each other. And at times, we teeter on dangerous. My stomach flutters because his words offer me the same hope, and it's the promise in them—I won't be abandoned. My parents, even in their presence, never wanted me. Being a widow, though it certainly wasn't Scott's fault, further cements the wounds from childhood. In Maguire, I find my protector and healer.

"Well, I'm not moving across the country, just across the driveway. Now, show me the progress." The contractors have hit some snags, but they are close to finishing. Maguire thinks I'll be moved in by the end of next week. And though I'll miss him, I believe we require this break.

The second we're on the landing of the steps, he opens the door and all the air escapes my lungs. I'm blown away by my home Maguire is single-handedly paying for. We walk straight into a hallway. If I were to turn left, we'd be walking toward the bedrooms. If we continued straight, we're in the galley kitchen and if we were to take a right, we're heading to the living room. Because the apartment is on the entire right end of the garage and is the whole length of it, my new home has tons of windows. The natural light is fantastic.

Maguire begins the tour. "The contractor took down a half wall in the galley kitchen and put an island to separate the two spaces. He used the same gray grained cabinets you picked out for the baby's bed. The small dormitory fridge is removed and in its place is a large double door stainless steel refrigerator." He points to the rest of the kitchen, as though he's Vanna White turning the letters on *Wheel of Fortune*. He's so adorable. "The backsplash is a slate blue subway tile. The walls have been repainted a calming light blue, one of your favorite colors I've heard, after purple. And the countertops are white quartz."

Heading down the hallway, he pulls back a closet door, or at least it's what it had been. Behind it is now a stackable washer and dryer unit. "The contractor didn't think he could configure it properly, telling me he'd have to locate it downstairs in the garage," he explains. I like this set up much better.

He continues the tour as if he's an agent on *House Hunters*, one of my favorite shows on television. "The first room is the master. It's not huge, but they were able to give you a small bathroom of your own. And because you love purple, I chose it for you." But it's more than just purple. It's the very shade of purple on the ends of my hair. The bed has been assembled. But what I fixate on is the design of the headboard.

"As you know, I've been working on a new line of headboards. And, you get one." It has stars etched into it like Maguire is designing for the crib. "I wanted to pay tribute to Scott with the crib. But as I'm designing it, I'm also making headboards with stars carved in them, too." Maguire wants some sort of symbol for Scott since he died protecting the stars and stripes of the American flag.

I walk back to the baby's room, not much bigger than a supply closet. "I wanted the baby to have his or her own space. It's not huge, but it's big enough for a crib, a rocking chair, and a dresser." I had picked blue for the room, knowing I'd decorate it Americana to continue the theme of the red, white, and blue.

Overwhelmed with my lip quivering, tears threaten to spill over. "Do you like it, darlin'?"

I don't think. I only react. I throw myself in Maguire's arms. "I don't like it, *I love it.*" And just like we had been a couple weeks ago, in his truck before Ned drove up on us, our lips are alarmingly too close to one another.

"Darlin'?"

"Yeah?" I ask, my head resting in the crook of his neck.

"You okay?" His voice dips down an octave or two. Am I okay? It's not a specific question. I mean, am I okay in his arms? *I'm too okay in his arms*, probably a little bit too comfortable. Am I okay while I'm taking in the deep aroma of his unique smell? As it's been since the day I hugged him at the funeral home, it's an earthy woodsy pine sort of fragrance. But since returning to work, it's the same but now combined with sawdust. Am I okay with his hard muscles in contrast to my soft curves? Am I okay that I feel his erection growing between us or that the wetness between my legs almost longs for him? I'm okay with all of this and because I'm *too okay with him*, I back up. Giving me space. Giving us space.

"Yeah, Maguire, I'm okay. I'm just tired all of a sudden. I better head back to the house, I think my bed is calling me."

I step away from his grasp. He doesn't stop me. I'm not sure if I'm grateful for this or disappointed.

Saturday morning rolls around. The California sun only has a couple more weeks of weather warm enough to justify a trip to the lake. My body, for a matter of fact, only has a couple more weeks of bikini wearing, too. Hopping out of bed early, well, early for me, I slip on my swimsuit and a sundress. Grabbing my large brimmed hat and sunglasses, I have my bag and towel slung over my shoulder. In the kitchen, Maguire is finishing up his boring breakfast. I've gotten an early start; he's gotten a late one. His eyes require a double take when he whips his head around a second time, zeroing in on my short dress.

"I'm heading to the lake for the day." I'm rummaging through his refrigerator, looking for easy snacks to bring. Maguire only has a few on-the-go kinds of foods, as he insists on cooking a meal each night. Moving to the pantry, I grab myself a can of chicken, attempting to open it.

"What in the world are you doing?" He's taking the can opener and chicken out of my hands.

"Making a chicken salad sandwich," I answer in my duh kind of way.

"Okay, you in the kitchen makes me a bit nervous." He puts everything up. "Listen, head to the lake. I'll be out after I get some chores done around the house. Maybe an hour. I'll bring lunch, got it?"

"I'm not helpless, you know."

He scoffs at me. The man dares to physically mock me. "*In the kitchen*, you kind of are." Giving him the bird, I'm almost out of the house, though I have a companion, Ranger, following behind me. I smile because his dog loves me more than him. Score one for me.

Popping my head back in, I'm in the mood to goad him a little. "I'm taking Ranger with me. I'm convinced he likes me better." Maguire has some half-assed comeback, and I ignore him, closing the door behind me.

Maguire

I pull up to my dock and the second I do, the hairs on the

back of my neck raise. Josh Elton is with Holland. He's known as a player around town and is standing over her in her very revealing swimsuit. I should know, it's the same one I remembered from the hotel several weeks ago. Josh is one hell of a craftsman. I snatched him up a year ago. He's probably one of my best, well after Teagan. But when it comes to Holland, he's about to see a different side to his boss.

"Hey, Mr. P!" Josh shouts, taking a dive into the water. Yeah, this riff-raff better fucking dive into the water.

I'm getting closer, leaving the cooler and chairs in the truck. My aviators are masking my scowl. Holland is sitting on a towel on the dock with Ranger, happy as a clam.

"You didn't tell me Josh lives right down the road," she mentions, surprised.

"Yeah, he lives with his mom, in her basement," I bite back a little harshly.

She cocks her head to the side, ignoring my snarky remark. "It's nice having someone close to my age, someone I can hang out with."

"Josh isn't *a kind of* hang out sort of boy, if you get what I mean."

She nods her head, watching Josh swim back to the ladder leading to the dock. "Well, that doesn't really matter, right, since I'm not that kind of girl. So no need to worry, Sarge."

Holland has this ability to call me Sarge when I'm a bit overbearing. Though I won't apologize since I'll run off every twit I think wants to get into Holland's pants. Waiting for the punk to pull himself out of the water, I call over to him, "Hey, Josh, want to help me with the stuff from my truck." Walking on the narrow hundred-foot dock, we get to the bed of the truck when my warning is clear. "Hey, I want to make sure we're on the same page. Holland won't be one of your conquests. You get me?" I ask.

His eyes widen as he backs up. "Um, Mr. P, I love women as much as the next guy. But Scott was my friend. Even I have standards and morals when it comes to getting some." He whips his wet hair to the side as water lands on my cheek.

"Good to know we're on the same page." I pull for the ice chest as he grabs the chairs.

Setting them up for us, he turns to Holland. "Hey, I better run. Have a couple errands before I head out for the night." He waves at her, but my daughter-in-law's glare is solely on me.

"Hungry? Thirsty?" I pull out a beer, popping off the top when I can't ignore the contempt on her pouty lips. Pushing up her glasses, she rolls her eyes, her arms crossed over her tempting cleavage. "What?" I ask innocently.

"You said something to him, didn't you? And let me guess, he told you he was Scott's friend." She pulls her own aviators back down on her face.

"Yeah. Scott hung out with him from time to time when he was here." I remember this. I mean, I like the kid, but my focus will always be on the promise Scott asked of me.

Her eyes continue to scorch me. "Did he also say how he came out to this dock the day he found out and got so drunk he slept here? Or how he sent flowers to the funeral home. I read every card and his was one of the most touching condolences."

Like stripping down a house to its studs, this girl has done the same to me. But I can't let her see me sweat. I have been working with what I'd known. Josh Elton is a man whore.

Her downturned lips are another indication of her mood.

"If I say I'm sorry, can we enjoy our afternoon at the lake?" I ask.

She's tapping her fingers on the wood of the dock. "Let's see, I'm waiting," she croons, her lips turning upward into a brilliant smile. This girl loves to see me eat crow.

Her perfect dimpled cheeks and the way her nose twitches when she wants something makes me ache for her more pronounced than the last time and the time before that. I extend my arms to her, and she takes them, bringing her up to eye level. "Darlin', please forgive me," I say the moment her face is in front of my own.

"Well, that's all I wanted." Her head is held high, proud she's gotten what she wants. "Now, we can enjoy our day together." She sits down smugly in one of the chairs Josh brought onto the dock. Her breasts are fuller in her bikini top. She's on the shorter side, but her legs seem a mile long leading to her bottom.

She fixates on the beer in my hands. "Fiddlesticks. Your beer looks so good."

This girl loves messing with me so much, too much. I seize this opportunity to repay the favor. I take a long swig of the cold brew. "Yep, it's what I need on a hot day like today." Sitting down close to her, she swipes at my arm, playfully smacking it, but shit, she has a nice swing.

"For a little girl, you hit pretty well," I tease, leaning over to retrieve something she can drink.

"Yeah, I'll get you, Maguire Parrish, don't turn your back for one second, I'll get you." She happily takes the lemonade.

"Should I lock my door at night?" I ask.

Tapping the bottom of her chin, she pauses, giving

me an *I'm in deep thought* kind of look. "It depends, but I'd sleep with one eye open."

"I'll take that under advisement." Turning to her, I attempt to delve into something more serious. "By the way, have you heard from your parents since you've been here?"

When Holland's upset, she tosses her head back, eyes closed as if she's taking in a cleansing breath. I give her time to answer, the ability to form her words. The hurt she displays from her pinching the bridge of her nose to a tear forming in the corner of her eyes illustrates this is a deep-seated pain.

"I texted when we got here, to let them know I made it to California. I texted Sarah before my parents to let Mark and her know we arrived safely." Her speech is shaky. "Can you believe that my best friend is more my family than my own parents?" She stops, her head turns down with her explanation. "I thought I'd tell them about the baby, but they'd only mention it to Christine if my mom bumped into her."

I have promised Holland I'll tell Chris but only after the first trimester. I didn't think Chris could survive if she was told about this gift and something happened. I know I wouldn't, and Holland would be destroyed.

"I'm sorry, darlin'." I want to pull her to me, telling her she'd never be alone again. I have her and I'm not letting go anytime soon. But is it a promise I can make? One day, she'll find someone who sees her, the whole Holland and will scoop her up. She won't be mine—she can't be mine. Until the day comes, I'll treasure this woman with all I have.

"I don't get it. I mean, this baby inside of me is my whole world. And I think it'll multiply a hundred times over when I hold him or her for the first time. Why can't they love me the way I deserve?" She turns her head away. " And it makes me wonder, how can I be a good mom when I never witnessed what a mom really is."

The pain in her voice settles into the pit of my stomach and I'm gripped with the same sadness. She's a part of me in some way. Maybe it's through her love for Scott or carrying my grandchild. Possibly it's simply because of the feelings she evokes within me. Her agony is mine.

I stand, only to walk toward her and kneel at her side. "Your love for your baby already is so evident. It's only going to grow. And though it's hard to think about, when you go without—it's how you know you'll do better than those shitheads you called parents." I want to wrap her in my arms, but I contain myself because the temptation is too high. "I need you to understand it's their fucking loss. You're the best thing in their lives and if they're too stupid to realize it, fuck them, fuck them all."

A wickedly devious smile peeks through the slits of her eyes. The shine and glimmer from her stare are always the indications something is coming.

She lets a little giggle out when she begins, "Yeah, fuck them, fuck them all."

"Ah, that's the spirit and I'll let this one slide, darlin'."

A broader smile than before takes over her face. "Yeah, thought you might."

CHAPTER 21

In the five weeks she's lived in my house, it's been so very comfortable with her, and I have loved every minute of it. I learned right away she's not a morning person. She can make a kick-ass cup of coffee but hates the sludge as she calls it. The color palette of her outfits gets crazier later in the week. On Monday, they're pretty muted, but by Friday they're plain loud. And unicorns, the girl is obsessed with unicorns from the many pairs of leggings she owns, to her wallet and hell, she has about fifty unicorn pens strung around my house. This brings me to another flaw of hers that should bother me. She's a slob, leaves towels all over the place. The girl can't cook to save her life. She drinks a gallon of orange juice like water and she plays her music too fucking loud. But her smile takes away my sadness. She sings beautifully as she walks around the house and she's easy to talk to.

When I get the all clear from the contractor that the apartment is completed, I'm sad to have my roommate moving out of my house.

I'm standing in the doorway watching her pick up the array of dirty clothes on the floor. "You want to wash them here?"

"Why? I can be a slob at my own place," she begins, and I stifle a laugh because she's right. Almost all the furniture is in the apartment. She wouldn't let me buy her a couch or a mattress. Using her first couple of paychecks, she had them both delivered yesterday. Plus, she has been stubborn about dishes, glasses, and silverware. Every day we get home, more items for her apartment are delivered from Amazon. With her flair for design, I'm not sure what to expect.

The table Scott and I made for her had been delivered weeks ago with other stuff she kept. The contractor and I moved all of it up the narrow staircase two days ago. She's waited to see the house completely finished from the last time I showed it to her a few weeks ago. She calls it the big reveal. The girl loves her surprises.

I take the basket of dirty clothes from her and we walk across the gravel to her new digs. "I can't wait to see it completed." She's squealing like a little girl and it's in these times I realize how young she truly is.

Opening the door to the long hallway, she stops, taking in a deep breath. Elise came over yesterday while we were at work. She staged the house as if we were on some HGTV show. She unpacked and washed all of Holland's dishware, displaying them on the island and the dining room table. It's bright orange with turquoise flowers throughout the design; a little too loud for me. But it's Holland through and through. The paintings I commissioned our in-house artist to create are beautiful. There's one of her and Scott on their wedding day. I didn't know how it would look as a painting, but it's priceless, as is the look on her face when she walks over to touch it.

Holland whips her head back to me. "This is all Mira, isn't it?" she asks.

"Yeah, darlin', she did all of them." The rest is a paisley print of blues, light browns and orange abstract prints. The long brown suede sectional is perfect against the wall of windows. What she's not expecting is the bench in the front of the apartment with a bay window.

"This is new."

I shrug. Yeah, it was my own special surprise for Holland. It cost quite a bit more, but when she mentioned she loved the same set-up at Ned and Elise's house, I knew I'd give her this.

"It's perfect."

On further inspection, she sees her own work in the apartment too. Elise snagged some of the pillows she made in excess for our in-house sales woman to sell. "Elise, right?"

My nod answers her. Her eyes then focus on the rocking chair I made her for the living room. It's a deep brown wood, matching the wood of the table Scott had made her years ago. The dining room table sits behind the rocking chair between the kitchen and the den.

"I can't wait to see more." She takes off and I follow her to the bathroom, sitting between the kitchen and her master bedroom. It's long and narrow with a tub for the baby, painted light blue similar to the rest of the house.

In her room, she'd already known the color would be light purple along with the frame I'd made. But Elise grabbed some of Holland's thousand thread sheets she makes flawlessly along with a duvet she'd designed for a client. Unbeknownst to her, it had been Elise who ordered it. The fabric is a deep purple with large daisies and lilies. In the room, Elise hung up more artwork by Mira. Holland touches every new item, walking around.

"The baby's room isn't finished yet," I mention. "The dresser is moved in there, still the same gray grain as the rest of the baby's furniture. We're still working on the crib design for a new baby division of the company."

"Maguire, it's perfect. I don't know what to say. And that sneaky little Elise, I'll have to get on her tomorrow when we meet for lunch."

Why does it bother me so much about her plans with someone else? And with Elise of all people? It's like I want her to rely on me to fulfill everything she needs—me and me alone. But that's tomorrow and today, well, we still have today. "So, this calls for a celebration. Why don't I cook for you? Or I can take you out. Your choice."

"Oh, fiddlesticks, I can't tonight. Teagan, Josh, and I have plans. We're celebrating my new place."

I'm not one to get my feelings hurt, but this stings to the core. I'd planned on cooking dinner in her new kitchen—if she wanted to stay in. Or I'd take her out for steak—that's something that puts a huge smile on her face.

Instead, I fake and fake it very well. "Oh, that's great, darlin'. You deserve a night out instead of hanging out with this old fogy."

She playfully hits me and again, there's nothing playful about the way this girl hits. "You're not an old fogy, not to me, Sarge, and you know how I love hanging out with you." She stops, looking down at the floor. "Maybe tomorrow after lunch with Elise."

"Sure, we'll play it by ear. Just be careful tonight and call me if you need anything. Don't want you out there drinking and driving."

Looking down at her stomach she giggles. "Yeah, well, the good thing about me is I'm the designated driver.

No one knows I'm pregnant, but I've told them I'm not drinking. It works well."

I lean in to give her a kiss on the cheek, telling her to be careful one last time. I leave and I've never felt more alone.

This could be a colossal mistake, but I've missed *her*. I've missed *her* a lot. I hadn't given much thought to the void she's filled in my heart. I don't want to fuck *her* just to fulfill a desire I'm not getting. I want to hang out with her. Picking up the phone, I hit her name on my screen and when I think it'll go to voice mail, she answers.

"Hey, stranger."

"Hey there, sweetheart." It's Kat and she's quiet, doesn't say a word. "Listen, I could come up with a million reasons I've not called you for the past several weeks. The bottom line is, I'm an ass."

She chuckles on the other end. "I feel bad calling you an ass with all you've been through but yeah, M, you've been a grade-A dickhead. I mean, I've tried to understand."

"I have some explaining to do. Would you like to come over for some dinner? But let me be straight up with you. It's not a hook-up I'm looking for."

"M, I don't do relationships, it's what I liked about you." Her tone is as even as it usually is.

"I'm not asking for a relationship, Kat. Maybe a friendship. But senselessly fucking isn't something I'm looking for. I mean, losing Scott, I have a new perspective... Well, shit, I didn't want to get into it over the phone."

She clears her voice. "Adeline happens to be at her dad's for the night. I'll be over in a half hour. But let me get this straight, no sex? Right?"

I chuckle at her. I've not known Kat to be this direct, but we've never talked much when we're together either.

"No, but maybe a movie?" I pause, wondering what her reaction will be.

"Yeah, M, I'd love to watch a movie with you. I'll see you soon." She ends the call and I go to the fridge, deciding to make chicken quesadillas. It doesn't seem right to make the steak I bought Holland—for another woman.

Kat is knocking on my sliding glass door about thirty minutes later. I'm done sautéing the chicken, adding the cheese and mushrooms to the pan. From the corner of my eye, I notice one of Holland's unicorn pens on the counter. I can't escape her.

In front of the window, I take in everything that's Kat Stephens. She's tall and a little too skinny. She has these rocking huge boobs she told me was one of her parting gifts from her ex-husband. She took him for all she could with his cheating ways and apparently an excellent boob job was one of them. She's always meticulous in appearance. Even if she's in a pair of yoga pants, she's a knockout. If I hadn't been left damaged and if Kat's ex-husband hadn't left her unable to trust everyone, we may have been able to build something. Of course, it doesn't help I'm falling in love with a girl I can never have.

"Kat." I open up my arms for a hug and she walks past me. "Well, shit, you didn't sound this pissed on the phone."

Her hands are on her hips. "Yeah, the more I thought about it, the madder I've become. We had a great thing, M, getting what we needed. Why change it? Why have you ignored me?"

I shrug my shoulders. "Things change, Kat. I mean, with Scott's passing, I have perspective. Guess you can say I want to have something I can build on."

"And this is your way of telling me you do—or don't—want it to be with me?"

Am I saying this? I can't have the person I want and I know this long-term. "No, I mean—hell, I don't know, Kat. But I don't want to lose you as a friend. If things progress because we care for one another and just not the next orgasm, then great, but if not, I want to keep you in my life."

Her pretty face tells me I'm out of the doghouse when her lips pull into a small grin. "You're a good man, Maguire Parrish." It's then, she hugs me. "Yeah, I don't want to lose you either. So, what are you feeding me for dinner?"

She makes herself at home, grabbing beers for both of us. After constructing the quesadillas, I sit down, and we fall into an easy-going banter back and forth.

It's a double-edged sword being out with people my age, but again I'm the only one sober. Josh invited his older brother, Jase, who's home from college for the weekend. He's a little older than I am. I can't help but notice he doesn't take his eyes off of me the whole night. He's good looking, better looking than Josh which I thought was impossible. Josh, in his own right, is the epitome of tall, dark, and handsome. With Jase, he's blond, blue-eyed, and built like a bodybuilder.

But it's uncomfortable, too. It's been less than three months since I've received the news about Scott. I'm not even remotely ready to start over—that is if I ever am. Plus, I have a passenger along for the ride, no one wants to be saddled with.

With Teagan and Josh on the floor dancing to House of Pain's "Jump Around," I'm at our table watching them. Teagan's turning the eyes of many on the floor, but as I've come to witness, she's very proud of her sexuality. She'll come straight out and say, *"You don't have the right parts for me, honey."* And then she walks away, leaving every man speechless.

Jase sits down, his cologne fills the air near me. It's so different than Maguire's. It smells expensive, a little citrus mixed in. His smile is one an orthodontist could trademark. "Hey, Holland," he says, talking a little over the music.

"Hey, look at your brother and Teagan go. If I didn't know them, I'd think they were a couple."

He begins to giggle and this little response of his makes him more attractive. "I'm going to tell you something and both Teagan and Josh would kill me if they knew I told you." I wait, this must be good. "Our parents were the best of friends. They both wanted Josh and Teagan to marry. I'm serious, if arranged marriages existed, they would have been betrothed. Both our moms decided they needed to be in activities together to strengthen the bond. They enrolled them in dance lessons."

I'm watching them move as if they own one another. I'm laughing at a young Josh and Teagan being forced into something like this. "I'm guessing they didn't take it well."

"Ha, if you knew our moms, you'd understand Teagan and Josh didn't stand a fighting chance. So, that's why they can move like that. They went on to win many awards together."

"Hell, they look like Baby and Johnny out there." I'm laughing so hard when I sense Jase's intense gaze on me. I turn away because I can't take it.

"Shit, Holland. I'm so sorry. I can't take my eyes off of you. I'm such an ass. I know you've had to have noticed."

Flipping my hair over my shoulder, I'm at a loss for what to say. I finally grab his hand, because he's turning redder and redder by the minute. "You know what, I'm flattered you think I'm pretty."

He laughs and I cock my head to the side. "Ah, shit, Holland, pretty doesn't even come close. If I cut out the freak factor, think we could be friends?"

Putting out my hand, he shakes it. "Yeah, I'd like that, Jase."

For the rest of the night, we watch Teagan and Josh out on the floor, taking it over with all their dances. We talk and talk and talk. It's healing being able to think of anything other than being a widow at twenty-one.

Teagan leaves with some long-legged platinum blonde. Josh goes with Teagan's girl's best friend.

"Well, I guess it's just us," I start when Jase loads into Maguire's truck, the Sarge insisted I drive tonight.

We're quiet on the way home and when I'm about to pass my turn to take Jase to his house, he starts, "Just go home. I don't want you going out of your way. It's still nice enough for me to walk home and I didn't get a workout today."

When we stop and say our goodbyes, I turn to

Maguire's house. I wonder if he's still up or what he's doing. Is he watching sports? Twisting my head, I first see her sedan and then watch the skank on the couch next to Maguire. It's Kat. Why do I hate her so much? Yeah, I know. She gets Maguire when I can't. It makes me irrationally mad. I want to walk in and mess with their night. But then again, he deserves companionship and happiness. I tamp down my jealousy and open the garage door leading to my new home.

In front of the bay window, I can see Maguire's house. Through the sliding door, I can tell he has his arm around Kat as she cuddles into him. I hate that I can see this—or—that I'm even watching them. At twenty-one, I'm falling in love with my husband's father. What's wrong with me?

Maguire is in my bed, rubbing my stomach, talking to the baby. I'm naked. His other hand is on my nipple. My fingers run through his hair. I'm smiling—I've never been so turned on. When his head turns to me, I can't hold back. "Make love to me, Maguire. I. Need. You."

His eyes are hooded, and his erection is hard against my body as he shifts around me. "Need me to take care of this for you, Sarge?" I croon.

He smacks my rear playfully. "Don't tease me like that, darlin'. You'll get punished." Oh, how I want him to put me over his knee. Did I just think this? I laugh when his mouth crashes against mine.

My eyes open briefly to an empty room before I catapult out of bed so freaking fast. I look around to get my bearings when I realize I just had the hottest and most forbidden dream about my father-in-law.

CHAPTER 22

Maguire

I t's lonely ever since Holland moved into her apartment. I'm making my eggs when a text comes through. Flipping them and reading the text at the same time, I feel a pull at my lips, smiling at the name appearing on my screen.

Darlin': I forgot. I have my first appointment today with my OB. I'll see you later at work.

This girl will not let me buy her a suitable car. She insists on driving Scott's truck until the life insurance money comes in.

Me: If you're driving to Redding, take my truck. I'll drive Scott's.

Darlin': I'm fine in Scott's truck.

No, she's not. I've seen her drive a stick shift.

Me: HOLLAND

I don't have to look at my phone to know her response.

Darlin': MAGUIRE

I'm out the door in just my running shorts as I'd

taken my sweaty shirt off the second I got home from my run and it's chilly out. I'm up the stairs and knocking on her door as a second text comes through.

Darlin': If you are at my door, you're shit out of luck. I'm not answering. Anyway, I'm getting in the shower.

Grabbing for the key I left above the door, I let myself in, swiping the keys she has on the table and replacing them with my own.

I'm on my way to work when I get a text. I'm smiling knowing her response will be priceless.

Darlin': That's it, I'm getting my locks changed, you asshole.

I pull over to respond, because—well, I just have to.

Me: I heard your landlord is quite the dick, I doubt he'll authorize it.

I'm about to put the truck in drive and pull out when a return text has me chuckling.

Darlin': You have no idea. The guy drives me bonkers. And he's sort of a control freak.

When it comes to her, she has no idea.

I'm at my desk when a knock on the door grabs my attention away from my new design. For years, I've been asked to make a crib. Now, I have the right incentive. Taking one last look at the sketch in front of me, I glance up to stare at the dark chocolate brown eyes of Holland.

"Hey, darlin', was just getting ready to call you."

Yeah, I've been worried about her. Redding is a good half an hour away and Holland's a horrible driver.

"Yeah, well, I'm here. I had to run to Target since I was in a city with one, finally. But I'll get with Diane to make up my time."

Shit, I don't care about her time but to be fair to my other employees, I don't say anything.

"I have something for you," she says. I look up, and I match the broad grin forming on her face.

In front of my desk, she's wearing a tighter outfit than she usually wears. Against the fabric of her bright purple shirt is the slightest swell in her stomach. I move my eyes to her face and notice more of her is getting bigger in certain places. I don't stay focused on her breasts but hell, they are there for my viewing pleasure. Shit, I'm a sick fuck.

She hands me over a black and white picture. It takes a second for my eyes to focus in on the words, "Hi, Gramps," with a little arrow pointing to a small bean looking image.

"Is this my grandbaby?" I question, standing and moving around the desk to be near her.

"Yes, Gramps, this is your grandbaby." I don't pull her; I envelop her into me. Today's scent is orange cinnamon. I bury my face in her neck. Anyone from the office staff could look up at any time and see us through the glass that serves as my walls. I'm sure they're looking intently. But this is my grandchild, Scott's little kid. I'm overly emotional now that I'm holding proof in my hands he'll be living within this child.

"Shit, darlin'." I wipe a rogue tear from the corner of my eye. "I'm so..." What am I? Happy? Sad? Excited? A little of everything. "I mean, I believed you before, but now, I'm holding part of Scott in my hands."

"I know, right? I'm unable to express how I feel.

How I love this baby so much. I'm right at twelve weeks. Which means I've passed the first trimester. It's a little overwhelming." She brings a shaky hand to her forehead as she blows a stray strand of hair from her eyes.

I stare down at my design, knowing I'll be finishing my grandchild's crib very soon.

An hour later, Ned walks into my office, no knock. It's how we've always operated. "Maguire, got a second?"

I'm to the point with the crib mock-up with measurements and a prototype on the drawing board. Ned stops in front of the picture of the crib, taking it in and then looks back at me. "I never thought you wanted to work toward a baby line in the past."

I'm standing in front of it. I want more for this crib, or at least for the crib that will sleep my precious little one. "Yeah, never had a reason to fiddle with one, until now."

He narrows his eyes at me. "Something you want to tell me. Is Kat…"

"Oh, fuck no." I walk around the large portable sketch pad in my room, putting the finishing touches on it. "But I still have a reason to build a crib."

"Holland?" His question is brief.

I nod. "Yeah, but she's not ready to tell anyone yet, so, if we can keep it between us. I can't imagine it'll be long before she has no choice—she's starting to show." Especially her boobs. I don't share this last part with my friend though. I try to force away these thoughts to anything but how she fills out her shirt.

"Well, that would explain the intimate embrace I saw you two in earlier." Yep, I know workplace gossip spreads like wildfire with an accelerant. "Is there something going on I should know about?" His hands are on his hips like he's a father scolding me.

I can answer his question honestly because nothing is. "Ned, we're close because Scottie asked me to watch over her. She's a great kid—a kid and my son's widow is all she is. I became overly emotional when she showed me the ultrasound. I mean, nothing can replace Scott, but it sure feels fucking fantastic to know he'll live on in his child." I rub the back of my neck, this conversation has me sweating, my armpits require new deodorant.

"Does Christine know?"

"Thanks, old friend, for reminding me I need to reach out to the devil with Holland now past her first trimester."

He chuckles, he knows Christine almost as well as I do. Hell, he had to pick me up off the floor at the hole in the wall bar the night she took Scottie from me—after my tattoo while I cried into every beer I drank.

His eyes wander to the new prototype of the crib when he continues, "Christine is going to be the most invasive grandparent ever. Think Holland's up for it?"

My thoughts are still on Christine and the conversation which I'm sure will turn into a blame game. I don't think of my response when I almost gush over Holland. "She's a strong girl. I think she could handle the world if it came between her and her child."

Ned raises his one eyebrow a bit higher. He doesn't challenge me, and I don't volunteer any more information.

It's the weekend. Doesn't Maguire know this? My text alerts keep on going off with his particular ring tone. After ten texts, I lean over the nightstand, snatching it up and dial his number at eight in the morning.

"Is there a comet threatening to end the earth, Maguire Parrish?" I bite out.

"Could you be a little less dramatic this morning?" His tone is playful, a pitch or two higher than it is typically.

"And it's for this very reason—it being the morning that I'm very dramatic," I reply, my eyes still closed.

"The day is wasting. Get out of bed. I have errands to run. It's better with company."

Ah, he wants me with him. Why does this brighten my day and warm my cheeks—and all the other things he affects—that he really shouldn't?

"Give me an hour."

"Make it half an hour and I will take you to breakfast."

I stretch out a little more in the hope it will wake me up. "You know the way to a pregnant woman's heart, don't you?"

I'm finishing the last bite of my pancakes when out of the blue, he begins, "I need to confess something." I notice a little of his *I'm guilty as sin* look crawling all over his face. It's easy to tell at this point with seeing him every single day.

"Oh, this will be good," I retort.

"Yeah, well, there's a reason I wanted to bring you out this weekend."

I'm staring at him when a small smirk pulls at the corner of my lips. "You mean, feeding your pregnant daughter-in-law isn't on the top of your list today—shame on you."

"Well, taking care of you, darlin', is always at the height of my priorities. As a matter of fact, one of the reasons I wanted to take you out," he pauses, taking another bite of his hash browns. "I thought we could start looking at a safer vehicle for you and the baby. You can't put a baby in the cab of Scottie's old truck. It's not safe."

I knew this was coming. He'd only dropped a million clues in the past couple of weeks. "Yeah, I understand this, but the baby isn't popping out of me tomorrow. I have some time. I haven't gotten Scott's life insurance yet so—I'm waiting."

"Then let's look. Okay? Just work with me."

What can I say to the man whose mission it's been to care for me? "Sure, we can look, but just look."

A smile appears on his face and I'm lighter than I've been in months. With our eyes locked on one another, I'm full of hope for what my future holds.

There are five SUVs and one minivan pulled up to the front of the building on the lot. When Maguire exits his truck, he's almost attacked.

"Maguire Parrish, it's so good to see your ugly mug." He bro-hugs this man in front of us. So it's right then, I realize it's not a casual walk through of potential cars. Maguire plans to buy me a vehicle today.

He turns to me, pointing my way. "This is Scottie's wife."

The man in his late fifties comes at me and holds his hand out. "Mrs. Parrish, I was so sad to learn of your husband's passing. Thank you so much for your sacrifice." I hate this when people say these words to me. I know they mean well, but my sacrifice? It makes it sound as if I gave permission for Scott to be killed at an early age. Sure as hell I hadn't. But I give him a little nod and thank him.

"Okay, missy, let's get you into a new car. I hear congrats are in order for you." He puts his arm around my shoulders, leading me to the various vehicles parked around the dealership. "Now, I don't think you've given any thought to a minivan, but I want you to have all the information."

I turn my head back to Maguire, who's smiling at this turn of events. I take my free hand, flipping him off. "You are in trouble, asswipe," I mouth and he only grins and waves at me. This man Maguire took me to is an out and out salesman, and I have a feeling I'm leaving with a freakin' new vehicle.

I'm following Maguire up the road in my brand-new Honda Pilot ready to spit bullets at him. When I told the salesman I'd fill out the paperwork for a loan, he only laughed. "Your car has been paid off already." I signed a couple of documents, and we were done. I wanted to yell at Maguire. I already owe him so much money from the trip.

When I get out of the car, we're not alone. Ned and Elise are in his house. "You think if you have company, I won't tear into you."

He cocks his head to the side. "Well, I won't lie, maybe a little. But first, let me tell you, I used some of the money I set aside for Scott to buy your car. It was Scottie's money. I still have some for the baby. It's a brand-new car, and I know you'll be safe. Please stop being so proud and take it, knowing Scott would want you to have it."

I wonder in my head how much money he'd set aside for Scott. The SUV was close to forty thousand with all the upgrades Maguire had insisted on. "Are you sure you have an account, and you're just not telling me this to make me feel better about it?"

He laughs, a belly laugh. "Sure, that's something I would have done to get you into a safer car, but I swear I started this when he was six. I'll show you all the statements. But there's still close to forty thousand for the baby, after the new car. I promise I'm not making it up."

Looking at my safe and brand-new silver SUV, I finally say the one thing I've not had a chance to articulate. "Thank you, Maguire. I know you're making your son very proud of the father you have been to him, even now that he's gone."

He stops, a tear falling down his face. Maguire is so hard on himself when it comes to Scott. He doesn't think he was the father Scott deserved but even with the many miles between them, he was the best father Scott could have ever asked for.

I leave Maguire outside to collect himself as I open the door to his house. Elise and Ned are at the table with a bottle of wine open. "Sorry, honey, none for you." I haven't told her yet that I'm pregnant. She stands, coming at me, her hands opened. "Oh, sweetie, I'm going to spoil the hell out of your baby." She cups my face in both of her hands. "I'm so happy for you."

Elise has stolen my heart. She always knows what to say. "Thanks, Elise." I stare at the wine, wishing for one second that I could drink it. But this baby inside of me is so much more important.

Ned stands, looking out the window. "I see he got his

way, got you a car."

"Well, that's the reason you're here, right? Maguire thinks having witnesses, I won't kill him."

Elise's loud pitch laugh startles me for a second. "Maguire getting his way, tell me it's not so."

It's then Maguire walks into the house and stops, all of us looking at him.

"What?" he asks and it's apparent we're talking about him.

"Oh, Elise has got your number, that's for sure," I add.

"Yeah, I'm sure she does, but don't believe a word she says about me. She's a terrible liar."

I'm shocked when the prim and proper Elise Landon flips Maguire off and we all erupt in laughter.

CHAPTER 23

Maguire

It's hard to believe Christmas is a week away. It's not improbable to get snow, but the weather has been hotter for December. I'm looking at the inventory for the new cribs which go to production after Christmas break. My crew is excited about this new line, I've drawn up plans for matching rocking chairs next. The lead carpenter is in my office, rechecking the designs.

"The dresser drawers/changing table combo is beautiful, too. Can we start on these afterward?" My mind isn't on what John asks me, it's on the baby and his or her mother. Speaking of Holland, I've not seen her today.

"Maguire, you hear me, man?"

I look over the table to John.

"Ah, shit, sorry, I'm in my own world. Yeah, get with Jolene. Have her gauge interest. I'll sign off on it if we get eight pre-orders." We rarely do pre-orders, except for sets, and with the nursery edition, we'll market it as a full set.

"Good to know. You did it again—it's going to exceed our expectations." John beams with pride.

"I'll start on it Monday when we return, the rest of you can start the next day." I always build the prototype. Of course, this prototype won't be sold. I have customers who only want item number one in the collection, but it's not going to be available. From there, my other carpenters make their own, and the differences can be seen in each individual piece. It's what sells our product.

After John leaves, I call down to the design house, and Diane picks up right away. "Di, is Holland in yet?"

When I don't hear the industrial machines in the background, my question is answered. Holland has those machines going almost the entire time she's at work. Her sheets have become our best-selling product from our design house. She makes impressive thousand thread count sheets individually for each order. We earn almost five hundred in profit for the sets. It's been a huge money generator.

"Um, no, she called in sick about a half an hour ago."

I'm out of my seat before I hang up.

"Irene," I call out to my secretary. "I'll be gone for the rest of the day." I'm out the door before there's a reply.

All my calls to her are going to voice mail. Inching up the incline to my place, her SUV is where it was parked this morning. I bypass my regular spot near my own house and leave the truck close to the garage. Taking the steps two at a time, I knock hard and loud on the door. "Darlin', you okay?"

"Come in." It's loud, it's Holland after all. I'm across the threshold of the door and faced with Holland at the long island separating the galley kitchen from the dining room. Her eyes are puffy and she's staring at an envelope. She hasn't raised her head to acknowledge me.

"What are you looking at?" I ask.

I sit next to her, but far enough away that I can't read

what it is. She scoots it over to me and as if a cold chill falls on her apartment, a shiver overtakes my body.

"It's what Scott's been reduced to. A check. A measly couple hundred thousand. It's all I have and once I cash it, I'm admitting he's never coming back." Her hands are on her head and I can't see her eyes now, but tears fall on the countertop.

My hand visibly shakes when I push it back toward her. I understand her hesitation and reluctance. "Darlin'..."

"Please don't say it, Maguire. I know it won't bring him back regardless of whether or not I cash this. He's been gone for four months. This is the final nail in his coffin. I just..."

I reach one hand to her shoulder. It's then she falls into my arms. We've been careful for months to avoid as much contact as we can. It's this unspoken and unwritten rule we waver on. Her hair is in her eyes and my shirt's already soaked with tears when her cries increase with each sob.

After my breakdown yesterday and with the check still yelling at me from across the room, I'm lost in an episode of Guy's Grocery Games when my phone rings.

Looking down at the screen, I smile. It's Teagan. I never know what'll come out of her mouth. Bracing myself, I answer, "Hello." I'm cheerful, as peppy as I can be.

"Girl! What's popping? Fuck, I missed you yesterday. I mean, Diane is nice, but she's old." I internally laugh because Teagan is missing what many people have—

a filter. "So, you puking? Have diarrhea? Fever? What the hell are we dealing with?"

She finally stops, letting me speak—I think. "Um, none of the above."

"Ah, you're too much of a goodie two shoes to play hooky. So, what gives, little mama?"

"Call it a mental health day…"

The line is silent. Teagan continues after a couple seconds. "Come on, girl, you gotta give me more to go on than that."

The truth is I've bonded with Teagan. I'm private, but I can share with her. "Yeah, okay, okay. I got Scott's life insurance check. And it was then I realized it's the last thing I'll get with his name on it. It's my last link to him." The tears begin to fall. I'm so tired of crying and crying and crying some more.

"Ah, shit bags in winter—that's a tough one, Holls. I'm so fucking sorry."

"Yeah, but I need the money. I hate cashing it though—when I do, it's over. And it seems even more real than it had when Scott's body was delivered back to the States."

"Holls?" Her tone changes, it's softer. "You know, the check isn't the last thing you have of him." I look down at my stomach, she's right.

"Well, listen to me—I'm a Debbie Downer. I know you didn't call me to get all depressed."

"Well, no, but I'm your friend, Holls, and I'll listen to you being Debbie Downer all day long if it's what you need."

This is why I adore Teagan so much. I close my eyes to savor her words, her vow to me as my friend. Plus she's as real and sincere as she is hilarious. "Thanks! I appreciate it. So, tell me the real reason for this call," I probe.

"Josh and I are going out for the night. Wanna come with? We're staying local, so the choices aren't many. I mean, I know you can't drink, but we can play pool and hang out."

"Um, sure—who's going?"

Maguire's company is small. About thirty people in all and it's pretty even age-wise, except there's only four of us under the age of thirty.

"You remember Jase, right? Josh's mighty fine hot brother home from medical school? He couldn't keep his eyes off of you last time." I choke on air and start coughing. "Hey, I may not be into men, but I still know a good-looking guy when I see one."

She's not wrong about Jase. "Are you going to leave me like you did last time if you find someone to take home for the night?"

"Ah, do I even have to answer you, little mama?" she teases.

"No, you whore, you don't have to answer me," I come right back at her.

"You know me well already. Now get on your dancing shoes and let's get ready for a fun night."

I'm in the garage, looking for the painting Scott and I created one time at a wine and paint night. The memory assaulted me after I had just watched *House Hunters*. The newlyweds on the show had their own paint and wine portraits hanging on the wall. I couldn't let it go. After finding them, I search the entire garage for a hammer. For a man who is a carpenter, it's the one basic tool I thought he'd have in his workspace.

Walking toward the house, I hurry toward Maguire's since I need to take a shower before I meet Teagan and Josh tonight. Knocking on the door, I let myself into the living room. But some noise behind the kitchen catches my attention. I walk toward the master bedroom. It's cracked. I'm about to rap on the door to let him know I'm in the house. Through the slit is a mirror, that reflects his image. I still. I can't think because, in the reflection, he has his very erect member in his hand, sliding it up and down. The moans and groans have me wanting to see more, for there to be more. Oh, shit, what am I saying? I can't even call *his thing* what it is. This man is my father-in-law and I can't refer to *his thing* as anything but his member. But I become wet. So wet, I want to shove my fingers down my pants. But I don't.

I continue to stare until his strokes stop and he calls out, "Hello?"

I run down the hall and don't stop until I get to my own home and lock the door behind me. What have I just done?

CHAPTER 24

"Hello," I call out. I look up and the door is cracked. I thought I shut and locked that motherfucker. Hell, there's really only one person it could be. And shit, from her vantage, she would have been able to see me from the mirror. I grab for my phone to call her. It goes instantly to voice mail. Shit, not that I should be ashamed, only it's her face I always imagine near my cock as she sucks me off, her purple ends falling all over my naked body. Moving over to the text function, I type in an angry and short way.

Me: Darlin', were you just here?

I stand to look at my window as she slips through the garage door. Shit, and she's running. It's not something she should be doing five months pregnant. I keep on texting her without a response. After an hour, a beep from my text alert comes through.

Darlin': No, I've been home all day.

Fuck, the little brat is lying to me. Well, I can handle many things, but we're adults, let's get this out of the way. I don't want her ignoring me as she watched me jacking the beanstalk and all. I step out of the front door, making my way to the garage, I'm at the door, almost banging on it. But she doesn't answer. I grab for the extra key and help myself into the house. The music is wafting through her apartment, one of those fucking *emu* bands I hate.

"Holland, come on, we're going to talk about this like adults." I don't hear her, and I work my way down the hall, now concerned.

I pass the hallway bathroom, to her own bedroom, where the door is shut. Knocking on her bedroom door, I hear an *"oh, fuck"* behind it.

Pulling it back gently, she's flushed. And she should be, when I saw her almost running across the driveway, she'd been going faster than she should. Or, maybe she still has these blushing cheeks due to what she's seen.

"Sarge, seriously, you make yourself way too at home in my place."

I don't hold it in, not for a second. "Yeah, says the woman who was at my house, helping herself inside."

Her hands are on her hips. "I told you I was here. I have no idea what you're talking about."

"Yeah, I'm sure you didn't get a good show either. Hope you enjoyed it." I wink and leave her breathless.

Holland

I still can't get over what I had witnessed. And more so, he confronted me about it. I lied and didn't even feel remorseful.

I'm putting on a little makeup and trying to find something that fits my protruding belly. I've bought a couple maternity outfits, but nothing is really my style. I've been living in larger leggings and shirts I'm able to pull off the racks at Target.

I decide on a pair of purple paisley leggings and a long black sweater dress. It would typically swallow me, but now with the baby bump entirely taking over my stomach, it's undeniable I'm pregnant.

I'm through the front door, heading down the steps. Opening the entrance to the garage, I bump into Jase. "Oh, wow, Jase, hey. I wasn't expecting you."

He takes one look at my stomach and I realize his brother has not shared the happy news with him.

He attempts to act all normal as if he's not noticed. It's like having a unicorn between us. It's that obvious. "I hope you don't mind me stopping by. Teagan mentioned you were coming, and I thought I'd offer to be the designated driver this time..."

I point to my stomach. "Yeah, as you can see—I have designated driver status for the next couple months."

Now he's staring at me—at it.

"Um, I'm sorry, I'm a dick. You pregnant was the last thing I expected..." He rakes his hands through his thick, blond hair. "Fuck, nothing is coming out right."

"Yeah, I get it. Believe me, it was the last thing I was expecting, too. To bury my husband and then find out I'm carrying his baby—I'm still working through it."

He opens his mouth to speak and nothing comes out.

"Jase, I get it. But friends, we promised to be friends. So, if you'd like to drive, sure, I'd love to hang out with you."

"Hell, Holland—you're one hell of a woman. After I've acted like an ass and all." He whips a piece of hair from his eyes as a big gust of wind hits us both. It has all of a sudden gotten a little colder.

I give him a little smirk. "Hey, it's okay." I link my hand through his. "Lead the way." His car is parked in front of Maguire's new workshop, which is almost completed. I try not to think of him, especially when gravel crackles under the tires of a car, making its way up the road. Jase is helping me into his BMW when Maguire opens the door, a scowl on his face, locking onto my own gaze while Kat gets out of her vehicle.

We're at a different bar, one of the three in town. This place, different from last time, is a pool hall with a dance floor. Josh and Teagan are dirty dancing. Every time they go to the bar to get a drink in between the "sets", they are surrounded by many girls. At this point, everyone in the bar gets that Teagan is into girls, just like Josh.

I'm shooting pool with Jase as we stare at the many women surrounding the dancing duo. "Do you think they do this to get some?" I ask.

"Oh, fuck yes. Those two are so alike. Players and two peas in a pod. They just happen to both love boobs." I'm laughing and we're the only two in the whole place who are sober. But it hasn't hindered me from kicking his ass at the pool table.

"Hell, Holland, you're good at this." He's lost three games already.

"Yeah, it's one of the many upsides of being married to Scott. We went out almost every weekend to shoot pool." With one mention of Scott, he's quiet. "I know your brother was close to Scott, did you know him?"

He shakes his head. "I didn't know Scott well. Josh

was torn up over his death. I actually came home to find him on the Parrish dock, drunk. The crazy motherfucker was lucky he didn't fall in and drown. For six summers, they hung out until there was this girl who took up all Scott's time." He says the last part, humorously. "Josh almost flew out for the funeral. Did you know that?"

"No, why didn't he?"

"Um," Jase begins as his color changes to a ghostly white. "Our dad died five years ago. It was sudden and it was hard. Josh found his body. After that day, when we watched our dad's coffin lower into the ground, Josh swore he'd never go to another funeral again. The sight haunted him."

We're still in front of the pool tables when a group comes over and asks if we're done. We walk toward the bar and sit at an open top table with just Cokes in our hands.

"Hell, Jase, I had no idea. Josh never talks about it."

"He never will." He looks up in time to catch Josh and Teagan waving at us, telling us bye. "It figures, those sluts," he begins, looking at his watch as I do the same.

"I hate to do this." I yawn. "But, can you take me home? This baby is draining me."

He stands, taking my hand. "Sure, Holland. Anything for you."

We're pulling up the gravel drive when I notice Maguire in the distance, close to Kat's car, giving her a hug. I'm glad we missed the kiss.

I'm just getting out of Jase's BMW and somehow the jerk has walked over from his house to the garage by the time the car stops.

"Holland," he begins, opening the door for me. "Glad

you decided to come home."

Jase is out of the car. "Hey, Maguire." He must not have heard Maguire's condescending words. "Would you like me to walk you upstairs, Holls?"

I'm about to answer when Maguire does this for me. "No, she's just fine."

I stare at the jerk in front of me and walk away, crossing in front of the car and giving Jase a big hug. "Before you go back to school after the holidays, let's do this again," I say. "You're a good friend, Jase." I open the garage door, attempting to shut it in Maguire's face. This doesn't stop him. He's behind me on the steps when I use my keys to open the door.

"I'm not in the mood to talk, you big jackalope," I begin and when I shut the door, he puts his stupid foot in the way and because he has his combat boots on, I know it doesn't hurt him. "Look, it's late and you've pissed me off, Sarge. Leave the lecture for tomorrow." My voice is louder than it usually is. Not that I'm quiet by nature, but I hope he understands how mad I am.

He walks in with no regard for my wishes. "So, that's that? You're moving on?" he demands.

"What? And you're one to talk—fucking someone just to get some? You have no right questioning me." I'm on my way to my room. When I turn around to him, he's on my tail. We are inches apart and I push him. "And how dare you question me when it comes to Scott. Fuck no, I'm not moving on, you asshole. Jase is a friend and I need one right now. And it's the truth."

He pulls on my wrist and brings me closer to him. "Oh, do you want the truth, is that where we are? The truth, Holland, because I think we both know the truth, right here—between us."

I push him again. "No, Sarge, I don't want the truth. Don't ever bring it up again, you feel me?"

His eyes physically wince. "Crystal clear, Holland. Crystal fucking clear."

After our fight from last night, the image of Maguire pleasuring himself is still playing in my mind. Hell, I miss sex, so much. After trying to get him out of my system watching some of my shows on DVR, I decide I need a bath. My en-suite doesn't have a tub, and I grab the bath salts and all I need, letting the water fill the tub in the hallway bathroom, leaving the door wide open.

I put my earbuds in and the sounds of Brendan Urie floats through my head. But even Panic! At the Disco can't remove the up and down movement of Maguire riding his own cock as I only dream of. I'm in my own world, but even as in the zone I'm grabbing my vibrator I'm glad I brought in with me. I'm dreaming of Maguire's mouth on my clit, I sense eyes on me. I sit up immediately, removing my earbuds in time to hear the creak to the front door alerting me someone was watching. I pop up faster than a pregnant woman should stand in a soapy tub. Pulling a towel to me, I run to the front window. Maguire is still on the gravel, approaching his house. With my phone in my hand, I watch Maguire slip through the front door.

Me: Were you over here?

And what can I say? I did the same to him.

Maguire: No, I've been over at my house all day.

And just like that, he lies, like I did.

CHAPTER 25

I wake to Christmas morning. It used to be one of my favorite holidays. I couldn't bring myself to put up a tree. I still have all of our Christmas decorations downstairs in the garage with the rest of Scott's stuff I've not had the heart to sort through.

It's been four days since I've seen Maguire, after our fight. When his truck pulls away from his house today and I'm positive I won't walk in on him, I slide into the front door to leave a check for the amount of money I owe him from our cross-country trip.

With the holiday shut down, I've not really been out of my apartment. I went shopping yesterday to buy something I could bake to take over to Christmas dinner at Ned and Elise's. Teagan swore I couldn't mess up this recipe she gave me. Starting the cherry-apple dump cake recipe, I follow the step-by-step directions. *"It's four ingredients, Holls—even you can't screw it up,"* she had claimed.

Picking up the recipe card, I laugh at her notes on the

bottom. *This calls for pineapple, but if anyone ever makes this recipe with pineapple when I'm around, I'll slit their fucking throats.* Classic Teagan. She must not like that fruit.

I take the can of cherry pie and apple pie mix, combining them to spread on the bottom of my Pyrex baking dish. I have the boxed cake mix, sprinkling it from the container over the fruit, topping it with a pound of butter, cut into small squares. I place it over everything in the pan. Baking it at three hundred seventy-five degrees for thirty minutes—well, this seems simple enough.

I walk into my bedroom and start wrapping my presents for Elise, Ned, Teagan, and even Maguire. Though I've not seen him, I knew right away what I'd get him for Christmas. Elise's present took lots of thought. We've been spending a lot of time together. She's become this surrogate mother I thought I'd never have. She's taught me simple recipes for when the baby comes along. I will, after all, have to feed him or her.

She has all these fantastic recipes she loaned me, to copy for my own menus. I took her favorites. They were easy to find since every meal she cooked a lot, were marked—*one of our favorites*. It took me ten days to type them up, making her own personal cookbook. I even enlisted Ned, having him grab some of her favorite pictures of the two of them. I made a collage for the cover. As I wrap it, I hold onto it a little longer because this woman has become so special to me. I sometimes wonder why she and Ned never had children. It's such a personal question and I'll never ask.

For Ned, I found a picture of Maguire and him in front of the warehouse when their business was big enough to move into a building other than their garages. I had it blown up, framing it in the same wood he and Maguire are constructing the baby line out of. I procured the services of

Teagan to make the frame.

For Teagan, I made her a unicorn hobo bag. She loves anything she can sling over her shoulder and adores unicorns almost as much as I do.

And of course, Maguire's gift is something I know he'll love. When my timer goes off, I'm pleased to see my cake is baked perfectly. I place it in this baking carrier Elise insisted on buying me one day on a shopping outing.

With my cake carrier and presents in my hands, I'm off to my vehicle. Maguire's truck is already gone. I'm curious if he'd stayed at Kat's last night, but after what I said to him, it's not my business. After all, we both have to move on.

Maguire

I've not seen her in four days, not since the debacle of the fight we'd had about Jase Elton bringing her home. I had wanted to admit what we'd been skirting around for the past four months. She shot me down.

Then there was the show I witnessed, her bringing herself to pleasure. Hell, I can't get it out of my mind. What's worse, I saw her vibrator. I mean, it was hot as hell but I should feel ashamed, right?

Then she snuck in my house when I left for Elise and Ned's this morning. I had to turn back around once I got to the main road, having forgotten my phone. The little brat left me a ridiculous check for three thousand dollars. I ripped it up the second I realized it was for our cross-country trip.

She's seen me with Kat, but she hasn't given me a chance to tell her Kat is only a friend. And Kat, I'm learning a lot about her. She has to know how I feel about Holland, but she never calls me on it. She's taken the role of friend seriously and we're better as friends than we ever were as lovers.

I pull up to Ned and Elise's earlier than I'd told them. When I ring the doorbell at eleven a.m., Elise is bringing me in out of the cold Christmas morning. "Get in here, handsome, before you get yourself sick." It's funny how quickly the outdoor temperature has dropped drastically, at the same time Holland and I have become frigid with one another.

Giving her an enormous hug, she looks behind me. "Where's Holland?"

"Oh, I'm sure she'll be here. We came separately today."

Elise has this way of looking at people, where she dips her head down yet raises her eyebrows at the same time. It's her spill it right now buddy look. But there's nothing to tell. Well, scratch that. There's plenty to say, but I don't.

She doesn't press anymore, only offers me a mimosa. "Hell, Elise, do I look like a mimosa kind of guy?" She turns to the fridge, grabbing me a beer. "Now, I'll never say no to one of these," I impart as I take it from her.

We're deep in conversation a couple hours later when others arrive. Ned and Elise open their home every year to anyone in the company who doesn't have family around. When a couple of our craftsmen walk in, I almost don't see her as she scurries into the kitchen. But her laugh is as irresistible as her smile. It fills the room and I turn to see her, in a pair of reindeer leggings and a long green shirt, with a big picture of Rudolf on the front. Her belly looks more significant than it had just days ago when I last saw her.

Behind her, is Jase and Josh Elton, both of them helping her with her dish and presents. Lord help anyone who eats what she brought, though Elise swears her cooking is getting better.

My mind races. Did Jase bring her? Did she meet him outside? I'd known the Elton boys would be here today. Their mom had gone on a cruise, leaving them alone. Elise wouldn't have it and insisted they come.

Holland is laughing at something Jase says, offering him a bemused smile. Her high-pitched and loud voice fills the room and my face begins to warm. When he puts his hand around her, my entire body burns with rage. "Green doesn't suit you." It's not the masculine voice of Ned. I turn to see Elise staring at me.

"I have no idea what you're talking about." She gives me the same look as before when I arrived without Holland. She walks away without any more input.

Several people are around the tree and various parts of the house with gifts for others. I watch from my vantage point when Holland gives a package wrapped in pink unicorns to Elise. The second she opens it, tears fall down Elise's face and she wraps her arms around Holland. I love how quickly these two have bonded. Holland needs it after the year she's had. And Elise, too, for that matter.

Ned's present is wrapped in pink unicorn wrapping paper also. He takes out a picture frame, then turns to Holland, encircling her in a hug, just like his wife had done.

When she looks up, her eyes lock on mine. I raise my hand, the same one holding my beer, in a casual hello. She points to the formal living room on the other side of the house. I take her lead, following her there, bumping into fucking Jase Elton. She may not be ready to move on, but he's ready to pounce when she is. I can see it in his eyes.

She's in the small TV room away from the heart of the house. "Merry Christmas, Sarge," she says, with a medium size package in her hand—again wrapped in unicorn paper. On further inspection, it's at least Christmassy. She hands it to me. I'd left her gift in this room, thinking I wanted to give it to her in privacy.

"Merry Christmas, darlin'," I begin. I place her present down when I turn to grab her box of goodies. "You look festive today."

She takes it, smiling at the wrapping paper. "Listen, Maguire, about the other day."

I lift my hand. "Water under the bridge, darlin'."

She closes her eyes, inhaling and exhaling deeply. "You don't think we should talk about it?"

"No, darlin', I don't think we should." Of course, I'm not sure if it's the fight or what I witnessed that she wants to finally discuss. It doesn't matter. I don't want to talk about any of it.

She looks down at her present in her hand. Sitting on the closest couch, she smiles, "Okay, if you say so." She unwraps the box, letting out a long and loud chuckle. "You remembered."

Does she not get it? I remember everything about her. She pulls out bottle after bottle of Bath and Body Works brand lotion, body wash, and perfume. I've bought her ten different new aromas they've started carrying in the past six months. "I love it." I motion to the box to let her know there's more. Pulling out a long and narrow rectangular case, she looks at it and then back at me. I don't say a word when she opens it up to find a sterling silver chain with an emerald dangling from the necklace.

"Maguire, holy hell, it's gorgeous—but it's..."

"Emerald, as you know, is Scott's birthstone. I

wanted you to have a memory of him always. And when the baby comes, you can add to it. You'll always have them closest to your heart."

She stands, crossing the space between us quickly. Giving me a hug, she pulls back hastily, staring into my eyes. "I can't go days without you. I don't like it when we fight. Please don't…"

"No, I feel the same way." I pull back swiftly too because her presence near me is too intoxicating. "Okay, let's see what you got me." Sitting down in the chair in the corner, I begin to unwrap the box, which happens to be a shoe box. I pull it back and I swear all the air escapes from my lungs. Inside are John Deere tractors similar to the ones I'd given Scott throughout the years.

"I couldn't part with the ones you gave to Scott, but I wanted you to have your own collection to show your grandbaby one day." Inside are ten different tractors. The way she knows me in such a short amount of time is almost scary. I don't think another woman has ever gotten me quite like she has.

"Darlin', it's perfect." She stands and I embrace her. But it's not just the gift that's perfect, it's the person who's now in my arms who absolutely *fits me* perfectly.

CHAPTER 26

Christmas came and went. I rang the new year in with a gallon of rocky road, crying for my husband. I'm still close to Maguire, but we've both drawn this invisible line we don't cross.

My baby bump is no longer a simple bump. It's a watermelon. I've been asked on several occasions if I'm having twins. Lesson number one in pregnancy etiquette— if you ask a lady how far along she is, and she simply answers the weeks and doesn't volunteer she's having multiple babies at one time—don't *fucking* ask.

It's only February and I still have eight more weeks to go. I'm not sure my stomach can stretch much more. I'm getting grief from Irene, Elise, and Teagan when it comes to the baby's gender. "It'll be so much easier planning a baby shower if we know the sex," Irene says every time I see her.

And the names—they want to know what I've picked out, too. I've kept tight-lipped about both names. They aren't up for debate and for this reason, I'll not share them until the baby is born. Since they're on the different side, I'm sure I'll have too many opinions. But they're the ones Scott and I picked out together, and I won't be changing them.

Elise has become my surrogate mother, going to birthing classes with me. Maguire wanted to be my partner. In normal situations, I may have allowed it. But since we've cut some of our contact with one another, it's easier to have Elise.

I'm listening to Panic! At the Disco, pinning the fabric together for curtains for the baby's room, when a loud knock has me lowering my music. With only one person it could be, I open the door to Jase Elton. He's not who I thought would be on the other side. A smile unfurls across my face. I've come to covet this man's friendship. We text often and he's the only one who has ever let me forget even if for a second, that I'm falling in love with my father-in-law.

"Whoa, girl, you weren't kidding when you said a watermelon."

He walks in with a large box in his hand, "Hey, gorgeous." He leans down, giving me a kiss on the cheek. "I thought I'd surprise you with what I've been told is the best baby gift ever."

"What in the name of Peter, Paul, and Mary are you doing here?" He's in medical school in San Francisco and it's a good five hours away. He doesn't come home on the weekends often because his studies are so intense.

"I know this girl. She's having a baby. So, I decided to deliver this personally." I attempt to give him a hug. "You're so cute," he adds. Though I can't get too close to him, his massive arms wrap around me.

"I'm as big as a house. I can't bend over. People keep on asking me if I'm having twins and I still have eight weeks to go."

He looks back and chuckles. "First, from this fourth-year med student, let me say, I can tell with one look at you; you don't look like you're having twins, beautiful. And second, you're absolutely gorgeous. I honestly can't think of anyone who is more gorgeous than you."

I touch his arm affectionately. "You're sweet..." I keep looking at the wrapped box in his hand. "Did you say something about a present?"

"Yeah, and afterward, I hope you'll let me take you to dinner."

I scrunch my face, sitting down when he hands me his gift. "I'm a pregnant woman, you want to feed me. Sign me up."

Tearing off a good portion of wrapping paper, I'm holding a portable swing in my lap. "I'm not sure if you have one yet, but this is portable. One of my friends who has just had her baby told me this is the best gift. She brings it to study sessions and her little boy sleeps through it all. It's not quite like the big old school ones, but I want to get something you will use. I researched all the reviews and they were good."

I'm absolutely touched. Though, touched doesn't cut it. Jase went out of his way to get me something different but would prove useful. I try to stand and I can't. He pulls me up and into a hug. My lips are close to his.

"*Jase,*" I warn. I'm not ready. But he makes it almost impossible to resist.

"Listen, Holls." I love he has a nickname for me. "I care for you—more than I should. Hell, I think of you all the time. Your name is the first one I look for on my phone every day, hoping to hear from you. But I know you're not remotely close to being able to move on. So, I'm friends until—or—if you're ever ready for more."

"Jase, why me? I'm a widow with a passenger who's not your responsibility. You're going to be a successful doctor and you're so freaking beautiful. You must have tons of women after you. So, I'm asking you again, *why me*?"

He winks my way. "Are you kidding? I have so many answers for you; however, I would be coming on too strong if I share them all. So, for now, why don't we just go get some dinner?"

I look down at my yoga pants and t-shirt. "Let me go change." I'm in my bedroom when the front door opens and closes loudly. I figure Jase has gone to his car for something. Exiting the bedroom in a pair of black leggings and a long black striped shirt, I'm starting down the hall when I'm assaulted with loud voices, just not one. Oh, hell, and they are elevated. There's only one other person I know who will help himself into my home.

Jase's voice is the first I hear. "I don't have any plans. I'm her friend. If it progresses, then it'll happen naturally, *Maguire*."

"You little shit, do you know what she's been through? You have no idea!" His voice booms through the house.

"*Maguire!*" I yell over the screams, as he's in Jase's face. "What in the world are you doing?"

"I came over here to see if you wanted some dinner. This jackass is making himself too comfortable here." Maguire's legs are in a wide stance. He's marking this territory as his.

"Maguire, the last time I checked I could have whoever I wanted in my own home." I turn my gaze to Jase. "Give me a second, will you, Jase?"

He nods, raking his hand through his thick blond

hair.

Walking down the stairs, Maguire paces in front of my stairwell. "Look, Holland, we need to set some rules."

"Um, yeah, we sure as hell do, Sarge." I stop, trying to take the scene from earlier in. "First off…"

He cuts me off. "No, my rules, I meant I need to establish rules, you live in my apartment. I set them, *my law*."

My hands are balled into fists. Maguire's nostrils flare and I want to punch him smack in the flipping nose. "Fuck you if you think those rules are going to stick for one second. But this should be good, so what's rule number one?"

"Listen, darlin', and listen good. I'm not paying for you to fuck someone in my apartment I provide for you. Scott's not even been gone a year."

I don't think when my hand makes contact with his face. "Don't you ever fucking talk to me like that again. And don't worry. I won't be fucking anyone in your apartment because I won't be fucking living here."

"Holland, wait." The pitch and the tone in his voice change as his hand reaches for my arm, but I shrug it off.

I walk up the steps, straight into my room, grabbing enough clothes for a couple of days. I leave the keys to my SUV on the counter. "Can you take me to Elise's house, please?" Jase doesn't say a word. He doesn't have to; he probably heard the whole sordid fight.

What just happened? I've never lost my cool like I have with

Holland. I'm watching from my window as Jase loads a suitcase into his BMW. I open the door, walking toward her but it's Jase who meets me halfway. "Let her calm down, Maguire. I know you care for her, but she can't take anymore." He doesn't let me respond.

"Where are you taking her?" I demand. The son of a bitch doesn't answer and keeps on walking.

I'm going out of my ever-loving mind when an hour later, headlights shine into my front windows. It's Ned. I guess I know where Holland is.

Grabbing two beers, I meet him at the front door, letting him in from the cold. He rubs the scruff of his beard. "I have two very upset ladies at my house, both fucking mad as hell at you. Holland is talking about all these crazy plans, moving home, moving in with Christine. Her exact words were, 'If I'm going to be controlled, it won't be by some fucking alpha wannabe male.' So, tell me what in the world happened?"

I go into everything—all the details from finding Jase to me issuing her an ultimatum. He puts down his beer. "Wow, you really dug your own grave haven't you, old friend?" I shrug, but we both know the truth to the question. "Gotta ask you—both Elise and I see how you look at her. Do you love her?"

Can I admit out loud what I already know in my heart? I shrug again.

"You know nothing can ever happen. I mean, I guess if there weren't a little one on the way, it would be different. But, M, come on."

"Of course my brain knows but tell it to my heart when I see the way that Elton fucker looks at her."

"Jase Elton is a good kid. And yeah, he's smitten with her—anyone with eyes can see that. Just as we all know there's something there between Holland and you. But, M, if there's anyone I could choose to help raise my grandbaby, you could do a lot worse than him."

Why does this send irrational shivers down my spine? Ned continues, "Well, I better get back to my gal. She's surely not heading the Maguire Parrish fan club today." He stands up from where we'd been sitting, patting me on the shoulder. "Give Holland a couple of days. Let her cool down. I'll give her tomorrow off, call it a mental health day. See you in the morning."

He's gone and I retreat into my kitchen, grabbing a bottle of Jim, my only comfort for the night.

I wake to something wet and cold on my face. My eyes open to the sight of my golden retriever. "Hey, boy. Glad to know someone's not mad at me." He's over at the door, scratching to go out. Attempting to sit, my gaze falls on the empty bottle of Beam. "Just a sec, boy," I utter, when Ranger continues to scratch and whine about being let out.

At the door, I have the sun blocked with a hand over my face. Opening the slider, he runs across the gravel. "Hey, boy, miss me?" It's the voice of Holland. She looks up at me, and I wave, like a fucking wave will get me out of the doghouse with her.

She flips me off, turning on her heels, heading inside. She has a couple of boxes and my heart drops. And what's worse, she's in Elise's Mercedes. First things first, I make my way to the sink and take four Advil. The banging in my head won't stop throbbing. But I can't let Holland leave without fighting for her.

On my way up the steps, the door is half open, but all

I can hear are sobs coming from the apartment. She's on the floor in the hall and my first thought is she's fallen.

"Darlin', you hurt?"

Her eyes shoot up at me. "Stay the fuck away from me, Maguire Parrish. I'm crying because I thought this was my place. Everyone has tried to control me, well, besides Scott. And now you issue me the *law according to the almighty Maguire Parrish*."

The slap she heaped on me yesterday did less damage than her words have now. "Let's get you off the floor first."

"No, go screw yourself." She leans forward trying to hoist herself on her knees, but it's not working. Her head is lowered to her chest and her chin tremors. With a look of defeat, she holds out her hands.

Pulling her up gently, she's in my face, when she pushes off of me. "Now, leave. Oh, wait, that's right. We have rules now, so don't worry. I'll leave." She walks to her kitchen and grabs a set of keys off the island, pitching them straight at my head. "Here are your keys. Elise is taking me today and I'll get my own car. I'm looking at an apartment in town."

"Holland, I was wrong. Please stop. I don't want you to leave."

She's down the hallway with one of the boxes, taking the contents of her dresser drawers and tossing them straight into the cardboard box. I'm in the doorway, watching it all. "Holland, what can I say to fix this?"

"Nothing, not one thing. I'm an adult and sure I'm young, but I'm not stupid. Do you think I would hop into bed with the first man that paid me attention? Jase has made no qualms about liking me, but he's become a good friend. You disrespected him and me acting like King Kong claiming me as your own."

"I'm jealous, Holland, you must know that. It's the same way when you see me with Kat."

With my speech rushed and stammering, she stops tossing shit into her boxes and steps in front of me. "Yeah, and when was the last time I verbally assaulted Kat, telling you who you can have at your house?" She gets as close as she can, screaming, and her spit hits me in the face. Her anger doesn't subside when she continues, "You used the one thing I need, my own independence against me. You used something to control me. Do you know how demeaning you were?"

"Yeah, darlin', I fucked up. Please, don't let this one mistake dictate the future you have. Don't leave. I'll agree to anything, *just don't leave.* I need to know you're across the driveway from me."

She looks at all the shit she's thrown into her boxes. "Well, it's not like I can carry this box down the stairs anyway."

"You'll stay?" I ask.

"I'll stay, but I make the rules. And you have to promise you'll respect them." Her hands are on her hips and she's so fucking darling—the whole reason for her pet name.

"I promise, darlin', just don't leave me."

CHAPTER 27

Josh and I are minding our own business in the corner of the breakroom when Maguire comes storming in. "Holland, I need to speak to you." His eyes aren't on mine when he orders me to his office. They're on Josh's. "And, you, isn't it time to get back to work? John told me you've been gone for ten minutes. Yep, I think your break is over."

"He was just getting up, Sarge." Josh's eyes plead with me. He might be scared of the jackalope in front of me, but I'm not.

Josh walks past him, taking a quick look at his watch, "Actually, Mr. P, I still have two minutes on my break." With Maguire's hands on his waist, Josh hurries past him with a simple, "Catch you later, Holls."

I'm laid back in my chair, my hand on my protruding belly. Thankfully, I have four weeks to go, but my hormones have taken over and I'm about to light into Maguire. I sure as hell don't plan to meet him in his office. "Was all that display of dominance necessary, Sarge?" I begin like I have not a care in the world. "I thought we went over this?"

He points to the seats in the breakroom and I lean back, not moving. He sits across the table, his fingers on his chin. Hell, why does one chin dimple have to be such a freakin' turn on?

"Look, I know one day you'll find another man who will fall madly in love with you. It very well might be Josh's brother." He pauses, taking in a deep breath. "You're special. Someone is sure to snatch you up." I want to object and it's on the tip of my tongue. "Just let me say my piece." I nod, giving him the floor. "It's hard to think about anyone but my son owning your heart one day. On top of it all, he'll become a father to my grandchild, too."

I understand his concern and I'll always be respectful of the promise he's made to Scott, but this has gotten deep, very fast. To bring a little humor back to the room, I put up my hand, now stopping him. "Dramatic much? First off, it'll be a while before I can imagine starting over again." Except in my declaration, I'm lying. There's one person I can imagine starting over with. He's right across from me. I put these thoughts so far out of my mind. "Josh is a funny guy. More so, he knew Scott. He was telling me about the time Scott worked here for the summer. And they snuck out and *your son* got so wasted."

"Wait, I don't remember this." Maguire cocks his head to the side, as Scott had done when he was confused.

"Yeah, I'm sure you don't. Anyway, the point I'm trying to make is I'm a big girl, I can make my own friends. And Josh is just that—a friend."

He stands, pushing the chair back. "But I won't ever stop looking out for you, darlin', you better believe it." He exits without another word. But what if I can only *see him* as the future he talks about? Again, I shake it from my mind before it has time to sink in.

Maguire

I'm enjoying a beautiful early spring evening, with a beer and my dog on my front porch. For mid-March, it's surprisingly warm. My mind is rooted in *The Hunt for Red October* when Ranger darts from his comfortable place in the shade. Looking up through my aviators is Holland. She has hit thirty-six weeks and I can't imagine her belly stretching anymore.

As she closes the space between us, I'm met with her flushed face. Immediately putting down the book, I'm next to her.

"What's wrong?" I ask, taking her by the arm and leading her to my deck.

"I'm not feeling well. I wasn't in the mood to cook. I think I may be hungry."

"Stay put, darlin'," I say, when she laughs deeper than she typically does.

"I'm nine months pregnant. You placed me in this low ass chair. It's safe to say I'm not going anywhere."

I'm away long enough to spoon up a fresh vegetable pasta salad and a glass of milk. On the deck, I have a great view of Holland's profile. Her cheeks aren't as flushed. She looks perfect. She glows. I've seen many pregnant women in my life, and none are as beautiful as Holland. She turns her head, catching me in the midst of watching her. "What?" Holland asks, pushing her brown hair from her face.

"Motherhood suits you, darlin'. Can't say that about

many women but for you, it comes naturally."

Pushing her head back, as she does when she disagrees with something, she purses her lips for a brief second. "You're kidding, right?"

"Not at all."

Tilting her head back, she laughs out loud. "I'm a mess." I give her the bowl of pasta and she begins to shovel it into her mouth. Between bites, she continues, "You're only saying this because I'm carrying your grandchild."

I kneel down next to her, placing my hand on her belly. "Believe me, this falls so far outside of the realm of simply being this baby's grandfather."

Did this come out of my mouth? I stand, raking my hand through my hair. "Shit, Holland."

Setting down her pasta, she attempts to push herself up, which proves to be impossible. I pull her toward me, and her belly is the only thing that stops us from crashing together. "I didn't mean to say it the way it came out," I begin to explain.

"But you meant it, right?" she asks as I look away.

I run my hands through my hair again, heaving out a large breath of air. "I've never denied it, you know this, darlin'."

"Yeah, that's what I thought." She hurries off and I don't stop her.

CHAPTER 28

The pain—it's like someone is burning me from the inside. Why does it hurt so much? I roll out of bed, it's the only way I know to get off of the mattress. Landing on my knees, I'm able to reach for the lamp switch, but I'm still on all fours. My gaze lands on the bed, where a large red spot catches my attention. Reaching between my legs, wetness assaults me. When I have my fingers in front of my eyes, I find I'm looking at my own blood.

Grabbing for my phone, I call Maguire. On the first ring, it's delivered straight to voice mail. His phone is always dead. I have no choice, I can't move. I can barely breathe. Pushing 911, I'm hardly able to state my address. The dispatcher stays on the line with me, talking me through breathing strategies—for calming purposes. It's ten minutes later when the sirens of the ambulance are barreling up the incline.

The dispatcher is still giving me techniques when a forceful push of pressure soaks my pajamas. No wonder I wasn't feeling well earlier the previous evening. I'm only at thirty-six weeks, but this baby is coming. The pain is so intense I begin to scream and I drop my phone, accidentally disconnecting the call with 911.

I'm still on all fours as the pressure builds. I wish I had told the dispatcher where my keys were or how to get to me. Shit, I only told them the address, not where they could find me. When the sirens disengage, it's less than three minutes before the door opens and Maguire is yelling out for me. I'm facing the opposite direction, but when his cries get closer, it's a split second before he's at my head.

"Darlin'?" he questions.

"The baby is coming!" I scream when one medic appears at my head.

"Ms. Parrish, hey, I'm Felicia. We're here to help. How far along are you?"

A contraction assaults me. With Maguire's hand on the floor, near my own, I take it, squeezing it as a comfort. "I'm thirty-six weeks," I almost scream in the first of what I imagine will be many contractions.

"Okay, we're moving you to your back and my partner, Leona, will be checking you." With Maguire's help, they assist me and I'm able to lie on my back, though it hurts like hell.

I'm quiet, my knees open to give the medic a great vantage point of everything under my hood.

"Um, Felicia," the second medic says to the first. "Can you come here."

I look at Maguire for the first time since he found me on the floor in my room. "Breathe, darlin', just breathe." He smiles, and I know he's as worried as I am, but he's my calm in the storm, the one to ground me in this moment of pure torture.

"Holland," the medic I know as Felicia calls to me. My attention is now on her and not my father-in-law. "Um, this baby is coming right now, hon."

My eyes dart to Maguire. "No, this *is not* the plan, Sarge. It's not what I've envisioned. Fix it, you've gotta fix it."

His fingers stroke my hair. "Listen, darlin', women have been giving birth to babies in their homes for years."

Felicia leans over my large stomach to make eye contact with me. "He's right, hon. I've delivered over a dozen babies. I have everything we need. If you can get me some clean sheets and blankets, we'll be good," she asks of Maguire.

Maguire stands to grab them. I pull him back to me. "Please don't leave," I beg. The other EMT stands and he directs her to the linen closet.

"Okay, the good thing is he or she's coming out the correct way. I see the head, it's crowning."

How's this possible, I wonder? I barely push, but it doesn't mean the pain isn't as intense as I've imagined. I take in one deep breath when the other medic rushes to my side with the supplies and a radio.

"Okay, Holland, I need you with everything you have—to push as hard as you can right now."

I bear down and push hard through the immense pain when I scream. No, it's not the word to describe what I do. It's noise, a loud as hell noise. My eyes stay locked on Maguire when a foreign cry fills the room. This time, it's not me.

"It's a girl!" Felicia yells over the commotion of my screaming baby. With the second medic on the radio and the first wrapping my baby in a white sheet, Felicia turns toward me, still on her knees, and only smiles. "The other ambulance is ten minutes out. Let me cut the umbilical cord." I'm sure it's a couple minutes but it seems like it's forever before the medic says anything else. "Okay, all done. Now, it's time to introduce you to your baby girl."

Maguire stands, grabbing several pillows to prop my head up off the floor. He then takes the bundled baby out of the medic's hands. "We will transport you to the hospital once the second ambulance gets here."

Her words don't even register when Maguire leans over, handing me the most prized possession my husband left me. One look in her eyes, I know she has the same ones of both her daddy and grandpa. Kissing her little forehead, I speak my first words to my girl. "Welcome to the world, Scotland May Parrish."

Maguire

Has there ever been a more beautiful sight? I've never seen one. Holland, with my granddaughter, doesn't compare to the majestic mountains I stare at from my deck or a sunset at the lake. This is beauty at its fullest. With the paramedics' assistance, I move Holland and my little Scottie to her bed. I sit next to them. Hell, I want to crawl into bed with both of these girls and hold them. But they're not mine to keep.

Scott would be brimming with pride. A mother holding her baby—his baby—I can imagine it now. *You know Dad when I told you Holland was it and I loved her more than my truck. It could never compare to her holding our little girl.* Scott hadn't been overly emotional, but he could be poignant and to the point. It's all the sentiment I would get from him, but it would be enough.

Since Holland announced the little one's name—I'd been teetering on the edge of an emotional breakdown as every sensation of the past eight months comes flooding back to me. "You did good, darlin'," I start, staring at her. Her own face is turned down, looking at her baby.

She tips her head up for the briefest of moments to smile. I've seen Holland in casual clothes, dressed up, hell, I've seen her in a bikini and she's never looked as knocked down fucking gorgeous as she does in this instant.

"I'm so tired."

I chuckle at her when she glances back at her baby. "Of course you are, darlin', it's hard work to give birth."

A smirk crawls over her face. I've seen this before and I brace myself for her sassy little mouth. "Are you speaking from experience, Sarge?"

Placing my hand on her knee, I continue to beam with pride at this mouthy little thing in front of me. "Glad to know that even in childbirth, you're still a little smart ass."

Before she has a rebuttal, the medic who delivered Scotland pops her head back in. "The second ambulance is here. They'll take you and Miss Scotland to the hospital together. Grandpa, you can follow them if you would like."

Grandpa, I love the sound of this title. I lean down and give Scotland a peck on her tiny little cheek. "I'll see you at the hospital, little darlin'." Giving Holland the same kiss, but more intimately on the forehead, I simply state, "Yeah, let me grab my keys and I'll be right behind you." Like there's any other place I'd be.

CHAPTER 29

Three things are weighing me down, standing in the door, watching Holland hold my granddaughter. First, I have to call Christine and I'd rather walk the desert without water than deal with her. Second, I promised Holland I'd get Scotland's crib set up before they release her tomorrow. But to do number two, I have to leave them for a couple of hours, which leads me to number three. I can't seem to pry myself away from these two.

I'm still getting used to Scott not being here. And Scotland, what a perfect name for her. She's everything I could ever want in a grandchild. But when her eyes open, I'm back to when I held my son for the first time. Her greenish hazel eyes, just like his—just like mine—are what causes the waterworks to fall freely. "Are you going to stand there, or are you going to hold your grandbaby?" Yes, this is much better than calling my ex-wife, who will be on the next flight here, probably on my fucking dime, too.

"You're ready to give her up, finally?" I tease, closing my distance between them quickly.

Sticking her tongue out at me, she's glowing brightly. "Now that we have been given the all clear and we know Scotland is safe, yes I am. But, only to you."

I've lived with Scotland as part of my world for five hours now. The pain, the loss of my son can never be genuinely erased, but this baby gives me hope Scott will live on in her.

"So, what do you think, Gramps, is she a keeper?" Holland asks.

My face is inches from this little babe in my arms. I can't speak. The air leaves me when every fiber of my being sees the future. In her eyes, I imagine the hours we'll play with Barbie Dolls or the snuggles on the couch as I teach her the ins and outs of college basketball. I may even follow the Tarheels now and give her a choice between UCLA or UNC. I can imagine the tea parties or the jewelry I'll allow her to decorate me in. Tears fill my eyes. Tearing my gaze from her to Holland, I finally answer. "Yeah, she's a keeper, that's for sure."

Sitting next to Holland, without thinking, I reach over and grab her knee. "You did good."

"Yeah, do you think you'll keep your phone fully charged from now on?" she sasses.

This girl—regardless of any situation she finds herself in, her mouth still is primed and ready to back talk. "Glad to know that mouth is still as vicious as ever."

Squeezing my arm playfully, her reply is pure Holland. "Yeah, but you wouldn't want me any other way."

True, so very true.

The second Elise and Ned burst through the visitor doors with pink balloons and roses, I pull my hand away from her knee instantly. There's a flash of fear in her eyes. As if Elise and Ned saw it, I stand quickly, giving my baby back to her mother.

After half an hour with all of them, I snag my friend to help with the furniture, leaving Holland and Scotland in the capable hands of Elise.

When we're in the truck, I wait for Ned to address one of the two things I don't want to talk about. "So, when are you going to call Christine?" he asks. I moan. It's one of the things I don't want to think about.

"Yeah, probably after we assemble the crib," I reply, quickly and abruptly.

He's nodding his head in the passenger seat. "So," he begins again, and I know in his long pause, he's about to bring up the number two thing I'd rather not discuss. "It looks like we interrupted a moment between you and Holland earlier."

I groan. "Just lending her some comfort. It was a tough day and scary—delivering in her house and all."

"Okay, you can pile that shit for someone else who may not know you as well as I do, but don't insult me by acting like I'm not your closest friend. I see you two together."

I grip the steering wheel tight, gritting my teeth together. "Yeah, and your point?" I bite out.

I watch him from my peripheral and he stays quiet for a while. Soon, he asks me the one question only he could ask. "You love her, don't you?"

Do I love her? Hell, I know the answer to his question. I knew it back in the truck on our cross-country trip. I knew it when we sat at the lake the first day here. It's been reaffirmed a hundred times since then. Fuck, yeah, I love my Holland.

"Shit, Ned. You know the answer as well as I do," I admit and it's the first time I've ever really even confessed it to myself. "I know it's wrong. Hell, do you think I want to love her? If I could will myself to love anyone besides her, I would."

"And Kat?" Ned asks.

"I've not been with anyone since Scott's funeral. Shit, I've tried with Kat—the day after we got back. It wasn't fair to her. I think she sees it and because Kat's a good woman, she's not fussed at me or even called me out on it."

"Well, my friend, as I told you a month ago, you've gotten yourself into quite the mess. And if I can see it and Kat has read it from you, hell, the second your ex-wife gets here, she'll see it as plain as day. More so, it's not hard to know Holland loves you, too."

I snap my head to the side. "What?" I ask dumbfounded.

"Come on, M, you have to see it, too. She looks at you as if you hung the moon. She adores you. She has this radiant glow about her when you're near her. I know the look of lust; I know the look of love. You can have lust without love, but when you love someone, you have both and as sure as the earth is round and the ocean is salty, that girl loves you, too."

"But we can't be together. It's wrong. You see it, right?" I ask, almost begging for his permission. With Holland, I see my whole self.

"I know what I've told you in the past. But you can't always choose love. But, yeah, I guess you're right, I suppose not. I mean, I get your apprehension." With his declaration, it's more proof why we can't be together.

I'm in the back of my SUV Maguire insisted on buying for the baby and me several months ago. He'd been right, that gloating jackalope. I remember how he got his way that day when he tricked me with breakfast and a trip to the dealership. He knew he won. And now that I'm enjoying everything of this car he paid for; he sure as flapjacks won.

"See, aren't you glad you have room now with the baby?" I'm in the back seat, Maguire turning onto the road that leads to our houses. I watch the up and down movements of my little girl. I can only think of the one thing I dread more than my next period and it's my mother-in-law.

"Does she have to come in tomorrow? I mean, give me a couple days to acclimate to being a mom. I know Christine, she's going to whip in, tell me everything I'm doing wrong, make me cry, leave me questioning myself, and threaten to come back a couple months later."

Maguire starts to choke on air. "Wow, darlin', you know Christine well. Yep, that's her MO. But the good thing, I bought her tickets for only three days. We just need to get through them."

I won't let Christine rain on my parade. "It's not like I have to see her day and night." I think of the time she'll be at her hotel and I'll get a break, somehow, some way.

"Well," Maguire begins, stretching out the one syllable. This isn't good. "She's actually staying with me."

My mouth drops. "Why in the flip flop polly wop is she staying with you?" I say it so loud I startle my poor newborn.

"Well, darlin'…"

"Don't freakin' *well, darlin'* me. What would provoke you to let her do this?" Tears free fall from my eyes. I'm not expecting them. They come even though I've not asked. I can't help the irrational anger overtaking me.

"Holland, calm down for one second."

"Oh, don't flipping tell me to calm down." We stop in front of the garage and I'm out of the back seat so quick. Leaning over, I unclip the baby seat from the base. Maguire is behind me and I whip around gently, attempting to keep my baby asleep. "Oh, no, you don't. You don't get to invite the mother-in-law from hell to question everything I do, then tell me to freakin' calm down." Opening the door to the garage, I hurry upstairs—leaving Maguire in my wake.

Placing the baby carrier on the floor, I slide down the back of the wall, allowing all the tears to flow after I tried to avoid letting Maguire see me cry. From my side view, I notice movement from Scotland. "Hey, little girl." This *is not* the welcome she deserves. I stand, taking the carrier and placing it on the table Scott made for me. Unbuckling her, I cuddle her close, walking down to the back of the apartment. Passing my room, I peek in. The blood on my sheets and the dirty towels on the floor are clean and gone.

The door at the end of the hall to Scotland's nursery is open. When I walk in, the pictures are hung. The crib and the rocking chair are assembled. The dresser Maguire made to match the crib has all the knick-knacks of Scott's set on the shelves above.

Opening the drawers, I'd expected them to be empty. I've not had my baby shower yet. In them are a dozen pink sleepers, several onesies, and a large bag of diapers. The red, white, and navy-blue stars are decorated around the room along with all the old Americana décor.

It's fitting for our baby to sleep under the same stars and stripes Scott died protecting. Scotland is starting to wiggle in my arms. Her little nose scrunches up and I smile at her. "Okay, little lady, you hungry? Let's get you fed."

I find nursing Scotland to be difficult, but when she

latches on, I pick up my phone.

Me: Hey, could you come over here? I'm sorry. I think I've found my sanity.

Within a second, he returns my text.

Maguire: Sure, darlin', no need to apologize.

His ability to take my crap causes me to giggle. Scott would have lost his ever-loving mind with me. Although Scott learned early on in our marriage that telling me to calm down elicited more anger from me than if he were to tell me I looked fat—he certainly would have lost his patience with me by now.

I'm in my own little world, watching Scotland nurse when I see something white from the corner of my eye. "I wave the white flag, I surrender!" he hollers from the other side of the wall. I grab a blanket near me, covering up.

"Hey, I'm decent, come in." He walks in looking for his baby. It's what he keeps on calling her. And honestly, I love it.

"Where's my little darlin'?" he asks. I lift up the blanket, showing her little foot when he nods, a blush covering his face.

"I'm only feeding her, it's as natural as taking a shit." Me swearing will clear the air because I will be chastised, and I'll act aloof.

Sure enough, when the condescending, "Holland," escapes his mouth, I counter with, "Maguire," and we fall into our usual banter.

He sits on the floor and I watch him as he watches me. It should be weird, but it never is, not with him. A thought occurs to me, "How late were you up last night making sure the nursery was put together?" I ask.

Shrugging his shoulders, he says, "Ah, this was nothing." Maguire draws his knees up to the core of his body. He's so humble. I love humility on Maguire. Hell, I love anything on Maguire, *or off of him.* Ah, fiddlesticks, what's wrong with me?

"And all the pink outfits?" I question.

He winks at me. "Who knew I'm so good at picking out baby girl clothes? I stuck with pink for now, but I'll get her an assortment. I even washed them for her in the baby detergent you have up here."

Be still my heart. Maguire did all this for me? "About Christine, I'm sorry. It's your house, of course, you should have her there."

He verbally groans. "It was what we did when Scott was young. She'd fly him out here and stay a day or two at my house because I always footed the bill. It was just easier in a way. But I should have been more considerate of you. After all, you're right, she'll be invasive and opinionated and overbearing and a lot of things that make Christine, Christine." He scrubs his chin and it's then I realize how tired this man is. He yawns when he continues, "So, I'm going to pay for a hotel in town." I try to stop him, but he puts up his hand. "No, it's already settled." He continues to yawn, and his eyes look heavy.

"Hey, go take a nap. I may need you later and if you're exhausted, that won't help me." Of course, I have no intention of asking for help, but it's one way to get him to sleep, which he needs.

"Let me get some shut-eye." He stands, walking to the two of us. He leans down, giving me a kiss on the forehead and he touches Scotland's foot affectionately. "Come get me if you need me and I mean it, Holland."

I wait to hear the front door open. It typically has this creak, but I figure he must have fixed it last night when I don't hear it. As Scotland unlatches herself from me and falls into a deep slumber, we meander our way into our living room to watch something, anything from my DVR. Rounding the small kitchen to the living room, Maguire is sprawled out on my couch, gently snoring. The gigantic man doesn't fit, but he's so freaking handsome lying there, snoozing away. I take one more glance at him before moving to my bedroom.

CHAPTER 30

Maguire

The second she's in my truck, Christine doesn't stop with the complaints. "Why can't I stay at the house? How am I going to get out to your place from town? I don't have a car. Great, I'm here and I can't see our granddaughter."

It's non-stop and my hand reaches for my shoulder, trying to work out the knots appearing with each new grievance. I let her go on for five minutes because history has proven I should never interrupt Christine.

"Shit, M, are you going to say anything?" Her tone is the same embedded in my head from seventeen years ago.

"Just waiting for you to finish, Chris."

Her hands rake through her deep brown hair, her eyes narrowing in on my own. "I've not even started yet."

Oh, and to think I'd been looking forward to seeing her again. "First, Chris, I'm going to let you borrow my truck. I'll drive Scott's truck while you're here."

"But, what's up with me not being able to stay with you? I mean, I always have." She's pleading with me. She wants as much time with our baby girl as she can get. I don't speak and she doesn't wait when she jumps to conclusions. "Holland doesn't want me there. She hates me. Oh, I see what it's like. I was willing to give her a home and she rats me out—making you excommunicate me."

A loud laugh emits from my mouth as sarcasm accompanies what I have to say next. "Always a drama queen, Chris." Her deadly looks, too, have not changed through the years. "Listen, I just need my space. I booked you a great room, my treat. You can come and go as you please."

She has nothing more to say but sits with her hands crossed in the passenger seat pouting. The thirty-minute ride is horrendous when we approach the town. Turning one direction takes us to the tiny town of Coral Creek, but the other way takes me home. "You want to run by the hotel or go straight to the house to see Scotland?"

"I guess we should go straight to your house since time with my grandbaby is limited." Oh, there's so much on the tip of my tongue. "By the way, what's up with the name she picked— Scotland May? What's with that girl and countries?"

Why am I up in arms over Christine trash talking Holland? It's obvious, the protective nature I have when it comes to her. After all, Christine is so much bark and a lot of bite.

My reply is quick and blunt. "Really, Christine? Scotland is in honor of Scott, our son. It was the one name they picked out early on. And May, do you even have to ask? It's our son's birth month."

I watch her head twist around so fast out of my side view. "Shit, M, you don't have to be such an ass about the whole thing."

"And I'm not going to watch you treat Holland like some second-rate citizen while you're here."

She slams her hand against the glass of the passenger door. "I fucking knew it. You didn't want me at your place. You think I'll pick on Holland."

"*You do pick* on Holland, Chris. You did it after she lost her husband, but you won't do it after she's given birth to our granddaughter, I won't allow it." My warning is clear. Though I'll limit my time with Holland, so Christine doesn't see what the two of us have together.

"And I lost my son, she wasn't letting me have a say in anything. Not where he was buried, not the songs for the funeral. I was left out of the loop of every decision."

I take in a deep breath before I go ape-shit crazy on her. "Listen, Chris, you can make this trip good or you can make it bad. Do you want to be a grade A bitch and push the mother of your granddaughter farther away from you than you two already are?"

Turning toward the road that leads up to my estate, the cab is so quiet I can hear her breathe. The second I stop, she's out of the door. "Go fuck yourself, Maguire." I chuckle. Glad to know some things never change. Christine is proof of it.

She makes herself at home, opening my door, peeking in before I can get out of the truck. "They're not here. Can you take me to her apartment?" She asks like she's not familiar with my home. She's made it her mission every time she visited.

"Follow me." When we're in the garage, she rushes up to the stairs, knocking on the door demanding access right away. If Holland's gotten the baby down for a nap, she's going to lose her ever-loving mind.

"Come in." Holland's voice carries. Of course, it

does.

Chris opens the door, turning toward her voice. We enter the living room space; Holland is in the second rocking chair I made. I follow Chris, her steps are hurried until she stops, turning around, pushing me back.

"She's nursing, M, you gotta go."

My face sours, in the way only Christine can cause. "Christine, I'm covered. It's fine. You both can come in. It's no big deal," Holland claims.

As Holland disagrees with her, Christine twists her body around, closing the space between the two of them. "Holland, honey, this is very inappropriate. What if he sees something?"

I want to come to her rescue, but I pause. Holland's gaze focuses on Christine. "Listen, nursing my baby is as natural as breathing. And anyway, it's just a boob. It's not like he's never seen one before."

I'm trying to hold onto my laughter. This is my girl. Team Holland's score is 1. Team Christine is at -10.

Holland

"Knock, knock." Christine's annoying, overbearing voice fills my apartment at nine in the morning. I've only just gotten to bed and she's letting herself into my home. I can only get Scotland to sleep in her swing Jase bought for me.

"Sshhh," I attempt to whisper. Christine has high heels on and they click-clack on the floor. "We've been up all night long. I finally just got her to sleep."

Christine focuses her sight on Scotland, who's snoozing like a champ finally. She crosses her arms, staring at my daughter in her swing. "Oh, this will not do, you can't let her sleep in her swing, how on earth will you get her on a schedule?"

Christine walks over to the swing, her hands about to turn off the back and forth motion.

"I will break your fingers if you stop her swing, Christine." I could blame it on the lack of sleep or the emotions of postpartum, but I think all of this only gives me an excuse to finally say what I've wanted to voice after all these years.

"Why, that's no way..."

"No, you listen to me. I'm tired, cranky, and doing this by myself. I'd love your help as long as you understand, Scotland *is my baby*. I call the shots. You want to hold her after she's slept that's fine. And as far as a schedule goes, she's four days old. Now, if you don't mind, I'm going to sleep. We'll be up soon, and I'll go find you at Maguire's."

She walks away, the click-clacking of her stupid heels only louder. I close my eyes and sleep the best three hours since before Scotland's birth. Is it because I'm overtired or that I finally told my mother-in-law off? I'm pretty sure it's the latter.

For three days, Christine has asked me how she can help. *"May I take the baby for a walk? Would you like me to hold the baby while you nap? Could I help with laundry? Would you like me to cook a couple of meals I can freeze for you?"* Now that I've set the record straight, I'm willing to let her bond with her granddaughter. Although the woman drives me bat crap crazy to the point of lunacy, she's a natural with Scotland.

We say our goodbyes, Elise and Ned volunteering to drive Christine to the airport. Scotland and I are outside waving when Maguire appears from his workshop. "I wasn't sure how this visit would go down, darlin', but you held your own and I think that old bat has come to respect you."

"The old bat. Do you think we can train Scotland to call her that instead of Grammy?"

A grin covers his face. "Shit, you just made my day with that little vision now in my mind." Like that, we settle back into our routine of the Holland/Maguire dynamic I've come to covet.

CHAPTER 31

I sometimes wonder if this baby even likes me. There are days she cries all the time. I can't seem to make her happy. And breastfeeding, I've come to find out isn't as easy as those lactation specialists insist, not for me anyway.

I walk around with Scotland all day long in the Baby Björn. When I sit down to rest my legs, she starts to fuss. Sometimes, I take her on rides in the car if I can't get her to calm down. I've shown up at Elise's house many times, asking her to walk around with her because sleep has not come to me in days.

Maguire comes over at seven. It's when Scotland really is raring up. If I thought she liked being held in the day, she demands it at night. He somehow can sit down with her and she lets him. But with me, the mother who has given her life, all she does is cry and spit up. Oh, and no matter what diaper I buy, she blows out of them.

She's six weeks old. It's the extent of my paid maternity leave, but I've extended my leave for at least six more weeks. There's no way I can begin work again when I'm not sleeping.

I still talk to Jase almost every day. But I've not seen him since Maguire had his bitch attack. The last time I spoke to him, he'd hinted around to surprising me soon.

I'm on my second mile, outside, walking back from the lake when I round Maguire's house to see Jase, leaning up against his BMW in his aviators. Oh, he looks sexy as sin. The second he spots me, he cuts the distance between us. I'm seeing something I don't get to look forward to much anymore when he gets close—adult interaction.

He must see it on my face. "Gorgeous, you look exhausted."

"I am. I'm so tired. If you take her, I could curl up on the gravel and fall asleep."

Putting his arm around me, he pulls me in tight. "We can do better than that. Let's get you into the house, give me the 411 on this little angel. Doctor's orders—you must take a nap."

"I won't even pretend I want to argue with you."

I turn to the alarm clock next to my bed. It's four p.m. I've been asleep for five hours. I don't hear a peep from the living room at all. But, hell, my boobs hurt so bad, I must find my baby and feed her. I'm up and out in the living room in a split second. I miss my angry baby. It's me and her against the world. Even with as much sleep I'm deprived of, my girl is my everything.

From the hallway, I turn into the living room and come face-to-face with a surprise. Maguire is on the couch, Scotland is lying on her own stomach, *on his stomach*. His head pops up when he hears movement. "Did you kill Jase?" I tease.

He smirks. "Jase's mom called. She locked herself out of the house. When he saw I was home, he asked me if I could take over for him. And quite honestly, I thought the kid was in over his head at first. As much as I hate to admit it, he did a good job with Scottie." His voice is low, but he's not whispering. How in the world is she sleeping so peacefully?

I sit down near him in the rocking chair when the tears won't stop streaming. He adjusts, sitting up, and Scotland stays asleep as he moves her to his arms, cradling her. "Holland, what's wrong?"

"She hates me, it's official, my daughter hates me."

"No, darlin', it's not that—she can sense your stress. But your little girl is going to worship the ground you walk on, I assure you."

"You think?" I ask, and he nods. "Why?"

"*Because I worship* the ground you walk on."

Maguire

I've accepted Holland will never be mine. No matter how much I want or dream of her. It's going to happen sooner than I may have expected. I know she's still not ready to move on. But the Elton boy has fallen for her and hard. And he's present—even though I still don't like it, not one bit.

After Jase brought Scotland over, the day he had to go help his mom, I've been more present daily, making sure Holland is getting some sleep before Scottie is up all night. Sometimes, I stare at her, watching the way she effortlessly loves her kid, with all she has.

I've heard her some nights when I'm over at the house as she cries herself to sleep. I'm not sure if it's for the father Scott will never be or for the dad Scotland will never know. Or maybe, like me, she mourns for the love her and I can never share.

It's eleven p.m. about two weeks after I've been coming over, taking Scottie for her to sleep. She approaches us quickly—a woman on a mission, with her arms in front of her breasts. I've been around her enough to know she has to feed the baby in this stance. I hand over my little darlin' and turn my head to give her time to get Scottie latched on properly.

"I'm decent, Maguire," she croons, and I turn my head.

"Hey, I've meant to ask you. If Scotland was a boy, what name had Scott and you picked out?"

She smiles a broad grin stretching over her face. "Scott wanted to name our boy Maguire after you."

The air rushes out of my lungs. I don't think I breathe. My eyes water and I'm speechless. I finally croak out, "Why? Why would he want to do that?"

"Hell, Maguire, if you don't know by now—your son loved you with all he had. I've told you Scott turned out to be the best man I knew because of you. And he wanted to honor you. We were going to call him M.J. for short."

I close my eyes, finally accepting I was the father to Scott I'd always wanted to be. Holland might not know this, but she's given me the second-best gift with her words. I've finally forgiven myself for not moving to Virginia. And I'm at peace with the father I was able to be to my son.

CHAPTER 32

Maguire

It's a faint sound wafting through my open windows. I can't make it out, but it's enough to instinctively bring my feet out of bed as they crash to the floor. I sling on my track pants quickly and a long-sleeved shirt. It may be May in California, but it's still chilly at night. On my deck, I take in the noise as it calls me to the garage. Making my way upstairs to her apartment, there's no denying the screams I'd heard from my own house. They are more prevalent now. I knock, but there's no way in hell Holland can hear me. Reaching above the doorframe, I find the spare key. Helping myself into her apartment, Holland's in the rocking chair I made for her living space.

"Darlin'?" I ask.

She doesn't flinch as if she senses my presence. Her eyes are full of tears as she holds the baby close to her body. Scotland is screaming so loud I can't hear myself think. She's not been the easiest newborn for Holland, but this time is different.

"I don't know what's wrong with her. She won't stop

crying. I thought we were moving from this phase. I've fed her, I've burped her, I've changed her." Holland is almost screaming for me to hear her over my sweet but deeply upset granddaughter. At eight weeks, Scottie is still not sleeping well. But the stubborn woman refuses to ask for help.

With three long strides, I close the distance between us. I hold out my hands, and she hesitates. "Let me take her," I offer.

"But I'm her mother. I should be able to comfort her." Her tears don't stop.

"And you're doing it by yourself. *You don't need to do it by yourself*, let me help you."

She reluctantly hands little Scottie to me. Cradling her in my arms, I walk around the small living room.

"You're already over here too much. *You do too much for us*."

I'm looking down and I'm instantly forced back in time as if I'm looking at my son twenty-two years earlier. I hear Holland, but I don't say anything to her, just Scotland. "Here, here, little darlin', I got you." I jostle her, just enough, strolling through the living room. Though her cries don't stop, they lessen. When I get her settled down, I take her and lay her on her back, bringing her knees up to her stomach, rubbing her small little belly.

I look up for a brief moment, Holland's tears still flowing down her face. "See, she hates me. You have her for five minutes, and she calms at your touch."

"Believe me, that's not the issue. You're exhausted. And I've done this before. Scott had colic. I'm sure it's the reason my girl is so fussy."

She's in my space in a matter of seconds, reaching for my baby. "Okay, now that I know, I've got it." She's practically sleeping on her feet.

"Oh, no, Holland Marie Parrish. Me and my little darlin' are heading back to my house. I still have her bassinet. I'll take a bottle and the diaper bag. You, my dear, are marching your butt back to bed. I'm on duty tonight. Not you."

"But, I'm still on maternity leave. You have to work tomorrow."

"Um, it's one of the perks of owning the company. So, there's that." I have Scotland in my arms and we're out of the door before she can argue.

I roll over and jump out of bed the second the clock near me comes into view. "Holy Shitake mushrooms!" I scream. I run into the bathroom, brushing my teeth quickly, rushing down the stairs and from the garage over the gravel driveway until I make it to the main house. Before I open the sliding door, I still at the sight in front of me. On the couch, Maguire is asleep with the baby on top of him. My heart tightens. For the first time after admitting to myself I have serious feelings for this man, I allow myself to see him as his own person and not an extension of Scott.

Carefully, I slide the door open as Scotland's little body starts to waken. I continue to stare at them both, a stunningly beautiful combination between these two, who encompass the most important people on this earth to me. With Scotland's wrestling body, Maguire starts to stir. The second his eyes open, they lock in on me.

"Morning." He yawns wide, pulling the wiggling baby to his body, grabbing her to sit up. He lifts her toward his face. "Morning, little darlin'," he begins. She makes this little gurgle sound, and I swear a small smile peeks out from behind her lips. "See, everyone's happy when they get a good night's sleep." He turns to me while I make my way around the front of the couch, sitting in the chair. "You doing better?"

"Yeah, I slept for seven straight hours. I can't believe it's almost ten in the morning," I begin, looking at his clock. "I feel like a brand-new woman." Reaching my arms out to take Scotland, I grab a blanket and settle in to feed her. It's funny, with Maguire, he's respectful when I nurse. Where most men would leave the area the entire time, he looks away for a brief moment and when the baby is latched on, I start a conversation with him.

When Scotland begins nursing, I ask, "So, what did you both do last night?"

"Well," he starts and points to the bassinet near the chair. "Scottie slept for a couple hours in her bassinet, letting her gramps catch a few z's, too. She woke up, took her bottle like a champ, and you should have heard the loud and long burp she let out. I'm surprised it didn't wake you."

I laugh because my girl can belch with the best of them.

I pull back the blanket, just long enough to see her almost black hair, kissing the top of her head. "Thanks for taking her for the night, Sarge, I didn't realize how much I needed a break."

He leans forward, putting his elbows on his knees. "Can you promise me something, darlin'?"

Cocking my head to the side, I cautiously answer. "Um, I'll try."

"I need you to call me the next time it gets this bad. You were on the brink of losing it last night. I'm here. I know you want to do it by yourself, but you don't need to."

I look away. I can't say it. But, leave it to Maguire to tackle it. Scotland unlatches herself and the second I lift her up to burp her, she lets out another loud belch. "Wow, look at you go." I stand and place her in the bassinet.

I still haven't replied to him.

"Darlin', what is it?" His elbows are still on his knees.

"It's hard, Maguire." It's all I say.

"You mean to ask for my help?" he clarifies.

I massage my temples. My eyes are closed. I can't look at him when I say this. "No, it's hard to be around you."

My eyes remain shut. I've never verbally acknowledged this in the past. I never could *verbally* say it out loud.

I open them only to have his eyes so close to mine, if I were to blink, my lashes would touch his.

"We both know what is between us—you know it, right?" I say.

His lips are mere centimeters from mine, his breath is hot on my skin, and he begins with merely a whisper, "Know what? That every time you enter a room, I can breathe again? Or that your simple smile makes the demons of my loss easier to take? I'm broken inside when I'm not near you. Maybe it's the second I can use any excuse to touch you, my whole entire body comes alive. Or is it, maybe just maybe I can't get you out of my mind ever?"

His hand touches my cheek and when I push the chair back so fast, I'm almost knocked over.

But he's not done when he continues, "So, if it's any of those things I've listed, I know. I know as the sky is blue and the mountains are high, my need for you is so intense, I can barely contain myself."

I can't breathe. I'm left speechless and I'm so lost at his proclamation, I fixate on his intense gaze.

"Holland?" His one-word question brings me back to reality, where he's my father-in-law and not the man I've fallen in love with.

"What do you want me to say in return, Maguire? That I question my own desires daily, of what it would be like to be with you? If I truly am falling for you because of you or is it because I miss Scott so much? That when I watch you with Scotland, I can see a future and a family I was cheated out of a year ago? That I question if it's you I love or the memory of Scott? Or that I dream about what it would be like for you to make love to me?"

He leans back, both hands on his head. "Of course, you'd feel guilty—it's all questions I ask myself. I sometimes think Scott will return just to kick my ass. But the heart doesn't choose who it loves."

"And are you telling me, you want to pursue this, pursue us? Be with your son's wife? Because as much as I've tried to justify it six ways to Sunday, I can't."

I'm on my feet, scooping my little girl into my arms—making my way to the apartment before Maguire can respond to this question because I'm not sure, either way he answers it, if I can handle the truth.

CHAPTER 33

Maguire

I've not seen Holland or my little darlin' for three days, not since our heart to heart. She's been avoiding me with every ounce of sneakiness the girl possesses. I had not been ready to answer her question if I wanted to pursue us because it's still wrong. No, fuck that—it's worse than just wrong. It's forbidden—taboo.

But I can't have her disappearing on me the second I pull into the driveway. I tiptoe up the stairs and gently knock on the door. I remember when Scott was a baby, it never failed, I'd get him down for a nap and the postman would ring the doorbell or a solicitor would stop by to sell me something useless. And it would upset his entire schedule for the day.

With a little rasp, Holland appears, her hair in a messy bun on the top of her head. She whispers, "Scottie is down for a nap." I love her calling her baby what I'd called my own Scott.

"Can we talk?" I ask with my hands in my jacket pockets.

"Um, sure, but not in here, wait for me on the steps. Give me a second, let me grab the monitor." She shuts the door practically in my face. Moving down the last step on the ground floor, I sit and wait for her. I don't turn when footsteps approach me from behind. A cold bottle touches my hand when she passes it to me. "I figured if we are going to have this conversation, we both might need something stronger than soda."

I take one of the Coronas and turn my back to the wall of the stairs, able to look at her as she does the same thing two steps above me, but on the opposite end, to face one another. "Can you drink?" I ask.

"Yeah, I'll pump and dump, no biggie." She says this as if I know what the hell she's talking about. Before I can question, she begins, "So, the floor is yours." She moves her eyes everywhere and anywhere to avoid direct eye contact with me.

"I miss you. You're purposely avoiding me." I'm staring at her as if it will command her to look at me.

She doesn't turn her head as she stutters, attempting to take the time like she's making sense of what is indeed in her heart. I've been around this girl enough. She's silently berating herself.

"I won't deny it, Maguire." She's still looking anywhere but at me.

I take in a deep breath, not sure I'm ready to say the words that need to be said. Or maybe it's more that she's not prepared to hear what's in my heart. I'm about to speak. "You asked me a question and I'm not sure I have a clear answer, not at all, but I want to try."

Her voice is barely audible. "And what was it I asked?"

"You asked—was I willing to pursue what's between

us." I wait for a response. I take this as some sort of indication she's ready to hear what's deeply embedded in my soul, I can't stand one second away from her presence.

"And? What's your answer?" Her tone is sincere, it's aching for permission as though I can go to the other side and ask my son's blessing to be with his wife.

"I honestly don't know if there's a clear cut answer, darlin', it's out of the realm of normal but hell, I hurt—I can't breathe when you're not near me. I need you like I need oxygen."

She moves down one step, right above me, leaning forward. "You don't think I want this, too? Your affection and dare I say, love for me, gives me the strength to put one foot in front of the other. But, it's not just me I have to think about, I have Scottie. What will she do when she finds out her mother's boyfriend is really her grandpa?"

Oh, how I love the sound of her referring to me as hers. "It's not conventional, but she'll be loved and it's the most important thing a child needs. I'll be there for her like I couldn't be with Scott and I'll love her mom deeply."

She's so close to me and rests her forehead against mine. "If it were that simple."

I won't lie to her. "You're right, darlin', there's nothing normal about this. It'll be hard. But we lost the most important person to us. A second chance at love rarely comes around. And we have it within arm's reach."

She's quiet, her one hand rubbing her temple and the other one dangerously close to my one hand as though she's warring with herself to take the plunge.

I break the awkwardness enveloping the whole garage. My gaze falls on the truck, Scott's truck parked near us, threatening to permeate my mind, shouting at me. "Do you think I want to love you, Holland? Do you think I want to crave you with my next breath, my next thought? I've tried to fight this, but hell, the heart wants what the heart wants."

It's with those last words I utter, she leans over and catches me unaware for a brief second as her lips crash to my own. Without thinking, I match her force, taking over as we find a rhythm, while my hands find the back of her head. My fingers work through her long brown curls. It's not long before her hand is around my waist. Without breaking our connection of our lips, I lift her gently, bringing her down the last couple of steps.

With us standing, I find the nearest wall or support, which happens to be a little supply closet in the middle of the garage and push her up against it. My hand roams her silky smooth legs. With her short shorts on, it's not long until my hand wraps around to her ass and it strays along her curves. A low guttural moan escapes Holland's mouth and she's given me all the permission I need. My hand travels up her back, and it's with only my fingertips. I unhook her bra. Another moan leaves her precious lips as my hand finds the front of her body and I dip my hands between the fabric of her bra and her breasts. They're soft to the touch and this time, I'm the one whose moan can be heard. I lean back, her eyes connecting with my own.

"Maguire." Her desire drips from her own mouth and my fingers move, beginning to unbuckle her shorts.

My gaze stays on her when I unzip her pants. "Darlin'?" I ask. She knows what I need, with my question.

"Sarge, do it. I want you. I've wanted you for a long time." I push down her panties, moving down her body. I'm in front of her, and I smell her arousal.

Her hands work through my hair, and I use one finger to open up her pussy. "Shit, you are beautiful." The wetness, she has to hear it as my finger works her clit.

"Sarge, please. Don't torture me. Please."

But this isn't how I want our first time. I want to sling her over my shoulder, taking her upstairs, making love to her the right way. But I can give her what she needs right now, a preview—an appetizer before the main course.

My finger circles her clit and her body shudders a little. I need to taste her. Hell, I want to burn it to memory. The second my tongue reaches her clit, she lets all the apprehension roll from her body. "Sarge, yes, right there. Don't stop, please don't stop."

"Hell, darlin'," I say as I pull away for just a second, "I have no plans of stopping." But with my tongue away from her clit, my fingers enter her. I plan to be inside of her in less than ten minutes when I can make love to her the way she deserves to be.

"Yeah, right there. Yes, right there," she continues to scream when my tongue finds her clit again. It's at this moment, her entire body begins to quake and I taste her release on my tongue. This is the start. It'll be hard, but the two of us together will be unstoppable.

She melts into my arms and I hold her on the bare floor of the garage, her bare and beautiful ass in my lap. Kissing her forehead, she turns her face to me, only smiling at me. "Do you regret this, darlin'?"

Before she can answer, a sound from the baby monitor has us both stopped in our tracks.

It takes a second to come out of the coma we're both in, to realize it's not Scottie crying. In one fluid second, the passion drains from my body like a flat tire.

"Do you smell that?" I ask, and we stand quickly, Holland pulling her shorts up to her waist.

It's more than the fire alarm piercing through the monitor. It's the smell of smoke that now billows and escapes through the bottom of the front door. I grab Holland before she can step on the stairs.

"Meet me below Scottie's window. I got her." I'm already up the steps, opening the door, the flames biting at me. I look back for a second as my mind is only on one thing—getting my girl, my baby. My heart is beating a million miles a minute. With one glance of the fire, I understand I'll not be leaving the way I came. Looking down at Holland, she opens her mouth to argue. "I need you underneath Scottie's window, *now*." I can't read the flashes of her eyes, but she runs one direction and I continue through the door.

I take one last look at Maguire running toward the fire. Flames are spreading through the front part of the house, in the living room. I'm below my daughter's room, there are no flames, though it's working its way toward the back, too fast. My heart is hammering. I pull out my phone I'd forgotten I stuck in my back pocket when Maguire had knocked on the door.

I'm screaming toward the room when the 911 dispatcher answers the phone. "My baby, she's in her room, there's a fire," I begin. "No," I reply to her questions on the other end. "My father-in-law ran in to get her. I'm below her window." As I'm giving her the address and the details, I hear something, a tap above. I look up to see Maguire, he's yelling something, pointing at me. Taking the phone away from my ear, I move from the window and out of the way, my view is on the glass when a massive crash hits against it.

My breathing hitches when I turn left of Scotland's room, where my bedroom is, and the flames are moving quick. With one more crack of the glass, one of Maguire's old end tables I'd stolen from him flies in the air and crashes ten feet from me.

He says nothing when the screams of my daughter permeate the early night sky. She has a sheet tied around her waist and crossing at her front, securing her at the shoulders, too. More sheets are wrapped at the back of her grandpa-made harness. I stop breathing, watching her suspended twenty feet in the air. The flames are less than ten feet from her as Maguire lowers my baby. The last ten feet, the progression speeds up. I grab her the second my outreached arms make contact with her.

"I got her, Maguire." I look up at his face, it's pitch black, as is my daughter's. Sirens barrel along the path to the house. I back up, he's got to jump. He has no choice as the flames are right at the window.

"Watch out, darlin'!" he yells. I wait for him to jump out when his body disappears from my sight. With my daughter in my hands, I look up to where the man I love was. In a split second, it looks as though the floor has enveloped him. He's no longer there.

Holland and Maguire's story continues in *Different as Night and Day* releasing August 8th.
Pre-order it now: https://amzn.to/2SgUWIu

A NOTE FROM THE AUTHOR
WHAT I'VE LEARNED ALONG THE WAY

Whisky, it's a drink I love immensely. But as I've used it as a refreshment for many of my characters in recent books, I've learned it takes on different spellings. Scottish whisky does not have the "e" in its name but Irish whiskey does. When the Irish immigrants brought whiskey to America, the "e" stayed. In this book, Maguire has Canadian whisky with Ned in his office. Canadian whisky too does not have an "e". But when he has Jim Beam, the American whiskey will be seen with an "e". But, all these crazy spellings won't deter me from having one of my favorite drinks.

~Leigh

IT TAKES A VILLAGE!

First and foremost, to the women who take the very rough draft of my words in the rawest form and treat it with the utmost care and respect. Nancy George—you've become my friend and I treasure you! Kymberly—you and your eagle eyes—I can't thank you enough for your help. Kelly Green—you are a great addition to my beta team! I can't tell you how much I appreciate the time and effort you took to help make this book a success.

Auden—you are my writing bestie and I couldn't do this without your support! I absolutely adore you. Thanks for being the voice of reason when my imaginary friends take over.

Amie—Holy Cannoli! I adore you so much! Thanks for your friendship and without you, I'd not be St. Leigh—I love it!

Ellie McLove—Thanks so much for the help on this book— with your guidance as I improved Holland and Maguire's story.

Emma—You are amazing! I'm so glad to be working with you again!

Julie Deaton—I'm in awe of your professionalism. I consider it a true honor to be able to work with you each and every time. Your work is top-notch! I couldn't write any books without you.

Najla Qamber—You continue to blow me away with each and every cover you design for me. I say it every time but this is the best. Thanks so much.

Give Me Books—Thanks for all the outreach you do for my books! It's fun working with all of you great ladies.

Angela—What can I say! I feel like I've found a gem in you and look forward to working with you more in the future!

Kelly—You've come in and blown my mind with all you do for me! You are such a help to me in so many ways. Thanks so very much!

Elizabeth—I tell you every story so many times, you know my characters as well as I do. This book has been no different. You are so encouraging, knowing how much my writing means to me.

Dawn—My best friend after twenty-five plus years! I love how much I shock you by my subject matter and how my ideas make you laugh. You always have my back and I can't imagine this life without you.

Succulent and Sassy Reads! You all are so awesome and I am humbled you follow me and encourage me to continue writing.

Thanks so much to my incredible arc team and to everyone who read an advance copy and posted a review. You ladies are so valuable to me!

I want to thank my readers because without you, this would not be possible!

Of course, none of this would be a possibility without the Hubs and our little ones who call me mom. I love you more than I can express.

~Leigh

ABOUT THE AUTHOR

Leigh Lennon is a mother, veteran and a wife of a cancer survivor. Originally with a degree in education, she started writing as an outlet that has led to a deep passion. She lugs her computer with her as she crafts her next story. Her imaginary friends become real on her pages as she creates a world for them. She loves pretty nails, spikey hair and large earrings. Leigh can be found drinking coffee or wine, depending on the time of the day.

OTHER BOOKS BY LEIGH LENNON

The Unbreakable Stand-Alone Collection:
Unfiltered (Justine and Nick's Story)
https://amzn.to/2MalyI4
Unacquainted (Rose and Brody's Story)
http://bit.ly/2Dz4kz1
Unwanted (Emma and Tyler's Story)
https://amzn.to/2HlidXZ
Unknown—coming soon (Ryan's story)

A Jake Davis Novella Series:
The Holiday Package https://amzn.to/2D4SL4u
The Sweetest Package https://amzn.to/2Haj4KN

The Breathless Series:
The Last Breath https://amzn.to/2AFkWWg
Continue Breathing (coming soon)

Stand Alone Books:
Stockholm https://amzn.to/2FpqVlS

Fans of Football Series:
Color Blind https://amzn.to/2wVfBbF
Rules of Submission https://amzn.to/2Hhbezg

The Power of Three Love Series:
Foundations https://amzn.to/2skCrGM
Fahrenheit https://amzn.to/2YEpF4z

PLEASE STALK LEIGH LENNON ON SOCIAL MEDIA

https://amzn.to/2u9s10t

https://www.facebook.com/leigh.reagan.7

https://goo.gl/dWw8pQ

https://www.instagram.com/leigh_lennon/

https://twitter.com/4leighlennon

Author Leigh Lennon's Website
https://www.authorleighlennon.com/

Facebook Group Page: Succulent and Sassy Reads
https://bit.ly/2DgMxgt

Made in the USA
Middletown, DE
23 December 2023